SEVEN WONDERS
JOURNALS

THE

PROMISE

SEVEN WONDERS JOURNALS

⊱THE⊰
PROMISE

BY PETER LERANGIS

HARPER

An Imprint of HarperCollinsPublishers

Seven Wonders Journals: The Promise

Text by Peter Lerangis, copyright © 2016 by HarperCollins Publishers
All rights reserved. Printed in the United States of America.

ISBN 978-0-06-223895-5

16 17 18 19 20   CG   10 9 8 7 6 5 4 3 2 1
❖
First Edition

~ THE ~

PROMISE

Wednesday, midmorning, in Mother's study

HE DID IT again.

Diary, if he were an enemy invader,[1] I would pluck out his eyes and march him through the streets naked on the back of a hose-beaked vromaski. But being that Massarym is my brother and my twin, all I can do is tolerate him. And complain to you.

I had a plan. It was going to be extraordinary. Ground-breaking! You know what I speak of, Diary. For all these years, I have *promised* to live up to my potential. I have written here, over and over, how I would stop *writing* all the time and instead *do* things. I would stop being so

---

1 Not that we have ever had any foreign invaders, but it is fun to imagine. Tomorrow I promise to begin my nineteenth short story, "Brave Karai and the Cannibals of Cakkiliskobos." Maybe I will think of a better title.

tongue-tied in front of people. Today I was going to show off the fruits of my months of research, my incredible new abilities. Atlantis would begin to know and respect its future king.

But—surprise of surprises—Massarym jumped in and ruined everything. No one will remember what I did today. And here I sit in Mother's dreary study, filled with strange liquids in old jars, stacks of books and parchments, equations written on the walls and all surfaces, and the half-collapsed skeleton of a dwarf griffin.

I was so looking forward to this opportunity. For the next week, our family is hosting King Sh'anar of the nation of Akkadia, along with his entire royal family and a delegation of viziers, ministers, and servants. Foreign visitors—here in Atlantis! For the first time in all my seventeen years! According to Mother and Father, we must impress the Akkadians as we enter this exciting new age— the age of Karai. At long last we will be ending our decades of isolationism, creating new diplomatic relations, sharing the fruits of our joyous prosperity. For too long we have kept to ourselves while other nations suffered, and this can only build resentment. Strong relations with the Akkadians would connect us to the Greeks, the Phoenicians, the Egyptians, the Hittites. We will become a valuable trade partner and ally to all mainland nations—a leader across the world! "Greatness cannot exist if nobody knows who you are," Mother has always insisted.[2]

I agree. And I have been working to revolutionize the special abilities of our family and Atlanteans in general. My hours in the laboratories with Grand Wizard Malarchos have—

No time for that. Mother will arrive soon. Where was I? Oh, yes. We all stood taking in the grandeur of the Parade Grounds, our newly constructed stadium. Tiered marble stands rose around us. The grass, carefully trimmed by an army of servants, stretched in all directions like a bright green tapestry. It rustled in the breeze under a blazing sun. Small clouds flitted across a crisp blue sky. As Mother explained the purposes of the Parade Grounds to King Sh'anar, translations were made by the plump Akkadian vizier, Xanthos. The vizier is a short, fat man with a pouchful of nuts and figs at his belt that seemed never to go empty.

This was my chance. A perfect time to screw up my courage and debut *my* greatness. To demonstrate what I, Karai, the next in line to the Atlantean throne, could do. By dint of my own hard work.

My moment.

I scratched the back of my head and took a deep breath. But before I could open my mouth, my brother took off into

---

2 Actually, it is entirely possible I thought of this. But I will defer to my elders and be glad NO ONE WILL EVER READ THIS BUT ME!

the sky like a cannonball. As far as any of the visitors could understand, he actually held a cannonball in his arms. He held *something* in his arms, that was certain. Something with extraordinary magic.

The Akkadian delegation gasped.

Mother smiled. Father looked dumbfounded.

I was astonished myself. My mouth opened and closed like a South Atlantean bottom-feeding fneepfish. Massarym whooped, a high-pitched "heee-oooo" that made him sound like a farm girl riding a sphinx for the first time. This action was so unusual, so against the laws of nature, I thought it might induce fainting or a mass fleeing. But King Sh'anar, dressed in rich blue robes that hung lightly on his shoulders, gave a deep, rumbling laugh. His wife, the queen, clapped her hands, as did Xanthos. The entire delegation followed suit.

Ever the gaudy showman, Massarym soared away, then turned back toward us as if cresting a steep hill. Without warning, he plummeted steeply toward me, a wild grin on his face.

"No! M-M-Mass— By the—" I spluttered, diving out of the way, tumbling to the ground.

My brother is reckless, headstrong, and possibly one of the biggest fools I've ever met. He also loves attention, and my mother loves to encourage him. Unfortunately, when your mother is the queen of the oldest, most prosperous nation in the world and you[3] know you're her favorite, well, you get to do things like discover some unearthly magic and use it to soar into the air in front of foreign delegations.

And humiliate your brother.[4]

"Karai! Come get meeeee!" Massarym shouted, executing a clumsy loop-the-loop with his thumb pressed to his nose and his fingers waggling in the air.

The juvenile gesture isn't what grabbed my attention. It was the glinting sphere he clutched with his other arm. As he flitted one way and the next, it caught the sun and flashed blindingly, and then completely darkened, then brightened again. The surface shimmered like water reflecting against a bathhouse wall.

All right, Diary, I can tell you are waiting for my confession. Yes, my brother's defiance of the laws of nature was breathtaking. Yes, any human being would have been, by rights, consumed with awe! But, yes, too, it is true that I was not so flabbergasted by these unearthly antics that I could resist sneaking several long looks at the Akkadian princess.

Arishti-Aya.

Such a name, Diary! It is sweetness and song itself. As for her beauty and wit, she could melt the heart of the foulest vizzeet. She was not laughing or clapping her hands like

---

3 Meaning Massarym.
4 Meaning me.

a child, as were the rest of her disappointingly dull retinue. She was simply smiling and watching politely. I felt a tiny surge of satisfaction that she wasn't so completely taken with Massarym's astounding display. Maybe I'd be the one to impress her with . . . my plan!

Yes! I had almost forgotten my original plan. In comparison to what Massarym had just done, it did seem a bit underwhelming. Still, when Arishti-Aya looked at me, I knew I needed to at least try.

Yes, you read that right. She actually turned and glanced my way.

O Diary, my fingers numb as I write of Arishti-Aya. Her hair lifted lightly in the morning breeze, revealing high, regal cheekbones. Her eyes crinkled at the edges when she smiled, and her dress was a shimmer of gossamer orange that seemed to wrap all around her without a single seam. I flinched as she looked at me, embarrassed at being caught staring. I began scratching the back of my head like crazy.

But as I averted my eyes, I saw that Massarym was gone—and in that moment the entire Akkadian delegation had pivoted to stare at . . . me!

Was I so transparent in my affections? I began to stammer an apology—of course, what else do I do but st-st-stammer?—but a roar of laughter interrupted me before I finished!

Were they laughing at me? No, Diary, it was worse.

They were laughing at an imitation of me—being conducted by Massarym behind my back! He hovered a fist's breadth off the ground, making fluttery gestures with his hands and batting his eyelashes. Of course—from the air, he would have been the only person to have noticed me staring at Arishti-Aya.

He was sitting on the shimmering orb, clutching it between his knees. As I turned to him in blind rage, he hooted with laughter. Did I take a swipe at him, as would have been my right? Of course not! I am a prince, and whacking the foolish grin off your brother's face is definitely not what you're supposed to do in front of foreign princesses.

Sorry. I meant to write, in front of foreign *delegations*. Yes.

"It's not polite to stare, Brother," Massarym said with a grin.

"Th-th-this . . . this . . ." O Diary, why do words fail to reach my lips when they are clearly in my brain? Why is it I articulate here, on parchment, perfectly well—but when I become exercised and angry, my tongue takes on the consistency of a rotten Atlantean goobifruit? ". . . is not a stare. It is a glare."

"Ah, yes, the precise writer with precise words," Massarym said. "Let me edit myself: it is not polite to *ogle* a princess. Let alone *drool*!"

"I was not—"

I held my anger. I would not let him bait me. I knew the Akkadian royal family didn't speak Atlantean (thank the gods). Still, at some point, verbal squabbling in any tongue becomes unseemly. So, calmly, politely, I forced a smile. I wore an expression on my face that said *Please forgive my brother's immaturity*.

But Massarym was not finished! Oh, not by the length of a Atlantean archer's mightiest shot.

"Allow me to show you proper princely technique," Massarym shouted, as he zoomed to the top of a magnificent fig tree. "First, using your magical ball of flight, you pick the most delicious, ripest figs and maybe grab a few flowers[5] on the way back . . ." He disappeared briefly into the Royal Garden to a chorus of gasps, then dived back to earth with both fruits and flowers in hand—directly in front of the princess.

Arishti-Aya exclaimed something in breathless Akkadian that I was very happy not to understand, as it had the tone and melody of a helpless swoon.

"Then," Massarym said, bowing low to Arishti-Aya as he presented his gifts, "you give them to the adoring princess, in exchange for her heart and soul."

I could feel my cheeks redden and my heartbeat quicken.

---

5 Yes, highly illegal and punishable—to all except the overindulged Massarym!

As I understand it, to the non-twinned masses this sort of embarrassment would be devastating. But to me? You know better, Diary. Our lives have been a daily battle of wits, Massarym's and mine. The bond between twins is a tangled knot, and my brain was attacking it with a million fingers. I would not yield to this juvenile mockery.

It was time for my plan. FINALLY.

I took a deep breath. And then I spoke. Plainly. Fluidly. In Akkadian.

"Ahu–i basu addanis . . ." I blurted out. *My brother is very . . .* The words were at the tip of my tongue. The word for *reckless* floated to the top of my consciousness. *"Kaqad-danu,"* I finished.

Ha! What an element of surprise, speaking in a tongue no Atlantean knew! How shocking and impressive! Now *this*, I thought, was vindication. Perhaps not the bedazzle-ment of flight, but bedazzlement of the mind!

The complete lack of response was not encouraging.

"A-a-annu?" I said. *Yes?*

Diary, I sense you are laughing at me, too. For expect-ing people to be breathless over my great skill. I grant you, this ability is not quite as flashy as flying around like a circus buffoon, yes. But these words have come to me through listening, not lessons. Through letting Akkadian words soak into my brain like seeds into rich loam, where they are fertilized by sound and context until they grow

11

into understanding. Vocabulary. Conversation. Is this not amazing?

Ah, still you scoff—but lo! The princess did no such thing. This young woman threw her head back with a musical laugh that showed wit, grace, intellect, and refinement.

The king, as kings are wont to do, expressed his great surprise with raised eyebrows. He then turned to his translator, and naturally I listened. I caught a few new words—*talmidu*[6], *xiaddanis*[7]—neither of which I knew before. The meanings unlocked themselves and took up lodging in my brain. It was as if a tiny librarian there were cataloguing them, shelving them, alphabetizing, building sections, and keeping watch over the whole lot.

"*Talmidu, achi ni.*" *Student, not me*, I tried. Which I thought would stand for *I am not a student.*

The princess laughed and corrected me. "*Talmidu ni-ai,*" she said, in a light and melodious voice, as if grammar lessons were the most enchanting form of Akkadian entertainment.

"Ah, *ni-ai*," I said.

Now the Akkadians began speaking to me all at once— the king, the queen, the vizier, and several courtiers, all quite taken with my display of linguistic ability. I was a bit overwhelmed at first, but I was also absorbing meanings

6 *Student.*

7 *Every.*

and sentence structure. And I was answering. Intelligently. It felt glorious. What I had done—all these bleary-eyed nights and ancient texts with ancient wizards—had permanently changed me!

My glory increased as I spotted Massarym out of the corner of my eye, now earthbound and positively smoking with jealousy.

"Well, then!" Father said. "I see you have been studying the language in preparation for the royal meeting, my son. Quite befitting a future king and diplomat."

Mother gave him a look I did not understand, then pursed her lips and smiled thinly at the Akkadians. "But perhaps," she said, "not the most exciting exercise for a stadium full of our devoted subjects, who cannot hear this conversation. I believe we test their patience."

I bowed my head respectfully. "Then shall we release the people and continue the royal tour?" I said in Akkadian. Seeing the frustration on Mother's face, I switched to Atlantean. "We haven't even s-s-s-seen things . . . the *libraries* . . . yet! And—and I c-c-can show . . . southern coastline is b-b—"

"I don't think so." Mother cut me off before I could say *beautiful*, taking hold of my arm with that scary kind of firm calm that mothers have when they are clearly angry about something.

I should have known Massarym would not give up

when ordinary, kind, considerate human beings would. Stepping in front of us with a grin that was pure deviltry, he exclaimed, "*Talmidu wackamidu!*"

Mocking the language of our guests with nonsense words! Wars have been fought for less than this![8] Naturally Massarym had planned another stunt, which would distract from this inflammatory act. So what did he do before our eyes? What would be even more impressive than flying or learning a new tongue?

He vanished—not a trace.

King Sh'anar, I thought, would have a seizure. His queen had to be held upright. I could hear a gasp sweep across the entire stadium, followed a breathless moment later by riotous applause.

I could not bring myself to look upon Arishti-Aya.

"Well! I am truly impressed!" King Sh'anar announced in Akkadian, which was duly conveyed in Atlantean by Xanthos the amply fed vizier.

"Thank you," Mother said, then turned swiftly to Father. "Uhla'ar, see that our guests receive the full tour, as I attend to scientific necessities."

"Yes, Qalani, my queen." As Father obediently commandeered the Atlantean delegation away, Mother grabbed

---

8 I do not know if this is a fact, as we have not experienced war in Atlantis, but my studies of other cultures demonstrate the incendiary results of such mockery.

me by the arm. "You and I need to talk," she said through clenched teeth. "Wait in my study. I'll be there shortly."

Which is why I sit here now, in abject misery, waiting to know what exactly I have done wrong. In my long, tedious wait, I think I shall amuse myself with a mental review of Akkadian vocabulary.

Life, dear Diary, is not fair.

Wednesday, late afternoon

SO, DIARY, MY good, quiet, secret-keeping friend, let me tell you how it went from the last time I wrote.

Mother burst through the door, scattering the Akkadian words to the distant corners of my mind. She sat in the carved wooden chair at the end of the massive table that dominates her study.

I stood.

"Sit," she commanded.

I sat.

"What was that, Karai?" She stared me right in the eyes. I can't meet her gaze when she does that; it makes me feel as if I'm lying—even though I have no idea what I'm doing wrong.

"What w-w-was what?" I replied in a voice appallingly close to a whimper.

"When a royal family of a large and prosperous nation

hosts another, there are some unspoken expectations. Simple ones, such as not murdering anyone, not declaring war without warning, making sure everyone has something to eat and drink. Luckily, we managed to meet all of those. However, we failed on another, equally important count. We looked foolish. Because of your actions. None of us speak Akkadian—your father and I don't have time to learn the language of every far-off nation that wants to be our ally. You've obviously put time into studying their tongue, yet you neglected to forewarn us of that ridiculous display."

I had been planning on telling her the truth—that I *hadn't* studied Akkadian, at least not formally. That this ability was achieved by changing the makeup of my own brain. That I had made a scientific discovery based on her work. But her words cut me to the quick.

"*RIDICULOUS D-D-DISPLAY?*" I burst out. "And what of M-M-Massarym—of his flying into . . . into the sky like a c-c-clown in a cheap magic show, of his stealing f-f-figs and flowers for the Akkadian p-p-p-p-p—"

"Princess?" Mother said with a knowing glance.

"D-d-disappearing into thin air?" I barged on. "Oh, yes, all of that certainly does not make us look f-f-foolish, does it? But I . . . Karai . . . speaking Ak-k-kkadian is *ridiculous*?"

"Massarym had my permission to do what he did," Mother said. "It was our way of unveiling the great wondrous power that has been the earth's gift to our continent.

You—you took us by *surprise*, Karai. It's an ugly position to be in. Did you think it through? Did you want us to speak to the Akkadians through you every time we had something to say? Did you want to be the translator, with your rudimentary knowledge, so that we would communicate with grunts and gestures and nervous laughter—this to a country for whom we seek to be guides and mentors? As we reach across the oceans, we must be careful. We cannot look like fools, Karai, and we cannot look like a family divided—which certainly showed in your behavior toward your brother!"

I laughed. "Oh, I see, Massarym had p-p-permission *to fly*! And it was perfectly fine for him to make a f-f-fool of me with cruel im . . . imi . . . imitations! What next . . . allow per . . . permission to turn himself into a vromaski and pass g-g-gas in front of the Akkadian royal family? What great wondrous p-p-power that would demonstrate!"

"Karai, must this conversation succumb to your reckless sarcasm?" Mother said. "Or can we still speak like thinking adults?"

I turned my back and pretended to examine the books that lined the walls. As you know, Diary, I hate losing my temper. I commanded myself to breathe slowly and deeply.

"What Massarym was doing," Mother continued, "was displaying our newest discovery, which will change the course of history for us and our country. Please control your feelings of jealousy toward him. You are seventeen now, almost a man."

This, Diary, was the sharpest cut of all—this use of the word *our* that did not include me. This word that referred to a discovery so great that nature itself had been changed. Mother is renowned and beloved for her genius in the scientific arts, and I have no illusions of her including me in all her discoveries. But Massarym? Now, I know my brother is not hopelessly mush brained[9], but, please, a scientist he is not.

"You . . . and *Massarym* . . . have a d-d-discovery together?" I asked with measured calmness.

Mother sighed wearily. "You and your brother are almost men, almost old enough to begin taking responsibilities in this government. The difference is that only one of you can be the future king."

"Me!" I blurted.

"Yes, my dear," Mother said. "Massarym is the *second in line* to the throne, Karai, owing to the fact that he was born ten minutes after you. Think about this, my son. Put yourself in his sandals and imagine how that makes him feel. So, at times, I let him in on a thing or two. At times, I indulge his desire to show off a bit. Give him these small things, please."

---

9 Note to any spy, foul-smelling thief, or twin who at the moment is reading this diary—here is written proof that I can indeed be fair-minded and kind toward my otherwise odious brother.

You give him all things, small and large, I wanted to say. But, Diary, I kept silent about this matter, and I hope you are proud of me. *Someone* should be proud. "And this discovery?" I said.

"It is about the rift that resides within the Great Onyx Circle," she said. "A . . . research project. Into the nature and substance of the mystical power."

"The rift?" I said. "The orig . . . begin . . . sor . . ."

"Source?" Mother said softly.

"*Source* . . . of all that makes Atlantis great?" I exclaimed. "Mother, the scrolls say—"

"The scrolls were written by backward-thinking old men who lived on fneepfish and wartgrass," Mother said. "We live in a different time, Karai. We have the capability of deep understanding. We can know *why* things happen instead of accepting them without question. Knowledge is ultimate power, and blind belief destroys civilizations."

This last statement was true, of course. No one knew this more than I. But the rift? Never in the history of our continent has anyone dared approach the source of Atlantean magic, besides the ancient priests who spent their lives guarding and worshiping it. For years they have lived within the mysterious circular ridge we call the Great Onyx Circle. It is possibly to traverse this ridge in places on horseback, but in recent years I feel the entire ridge has begun to rise, as if protecting the rift. I wonder if the priests are doing this with their odd magic powers. "And what of R'amphos and the scholars of the rift—"

"I work with them, my son," Mother said. "Their knowledge guides me. Together we have analyzed the structure of this energy. We have invented a way to sequester elements of its power into seven containers."

"Why on earth—?" I began.

"To preserve and to spread," Mother replied. "We are no longer the only civilization that uses the seas to travel great distances. Other countries have discovered Atlantis, and many envy what we possess. How long will it be before they try to take it away, before they invade and attempt to conquer?"

"So we s-s-steal away the energy in these—these—"

"Loculi," Mother said. "And, no, we don't steal. We stay where we are. No, Karai, with the ability to capture the components of energy, we can perhaps *give* them as offerings of peace. What better way to fend off invaders than to take away the need to invade? And they, too, will discover what our magic does to the air and to the earth and to the thoughts of men and women. Others will experience the wisdom and equality and peace that we have taken for granted."

"What does this have to do with M-M-Massarym's display?" I said. "I did not see w-w-w-wisdom and equality at the stadium, Mother . . . but terrible, unnatural w-w-wizardry!"

Mother was grinning now. "Ah, this is an unexpected result of our efforts, Karai. All we wanted to do was contain the elements of the energy. To be able to transport them and re-create them if need be. But, to our delight, we found that each Loculus conveyed its own specific power on contact."

"And it is *this* you want to give others?" I asked. "They will abuse these powers, Mother. They will attack us—"

Mother put her finger on my lips. "You must trust me, Karai. Only those with the blood of the royal family can activate these orbs. I have engineered them that way. Yes—in my laboratory I isolated special markers within our own blood and designed the Loculi to respond to them." She beamed with pride at her own accomplishment

I immediately felt myself blush. Yes, yes, Diary, I do indeed know about these markers. I did not mean to see her notes, but she leaves them around the lab, and what can she expect? Still, I never imagined this use for them! "Flying . . . invisibility . . ." I said, scratching nervously behind my ears, "these are extraordinary p-p-powers."

"Also superhuman strength . . . and a power that accelerates the body's healing beyond the reach of either natural regeneration or modern medicine and science . . . the ability to transport oneself from one place to another instantly . . ." Mother gave me a deep, penetrating look. "And this is, ultimately, why we are here. Because I would like to know, dear Karai, are you *truly* surprised at this news—or have you known about these Loculi?"

"H-H-How would I—?" I sputtered. "Of course not!"

"Because one of the Locular powers is the ability to understand other tongues," Mother barreled on.

Yes, Diary. The plot, shall we say, thickly grows.

"So you . . . s-s-susp . . . think I've stolen this energy?" I said.

"I might have given you permission to use it, had you asked," Mother said. "I gave Massarym permission to demonstrate one of them—"

"Two of them!" I said.

"One," Mother said. "I was not happy he used the Loculus of Invisibility."

"Rest assured, Mother, I know . . . knew . . . n-n-nothing about . . . Loculi," I said, "because this ability with f-f-foreign s-s-speech is . . . my own."

"Then it is even more spectacular," Mother said with a smile. "And I will rest assured."

With that, she dismissed me. But as I left, the last thing she said was, "I will include you from now on, my son. Perhaps tomorrow you can join me at the rift."

"Thank you, Mother!" I said.

"Along with your father," she said. "And Massarym, of course."

"Of c-c-course," I said through gritted teeth.

Progress, as they say, is often slow. But it is progress nonetheless.

Diary, I confess. I cannot wait.

* * *

Wednesday night, racing the sunrise

SLEEP HAS ABANDONED me. Writing will help.

You are saying that I lied to Mother, dear Diary. I imagine you wagging a finger at me. THIS IS KEEPING ME AWAKE!

But it is the truth—the ability to learn languages is indeed "my own"!

I did not have to tell her exactly how I got it.

I admit that hours after our discussion in my chambers, I am still a bit stung by her accusation, but I want to know everything. How did she build these containers she calls Loculi, and how did she cause the markers in our blood to activate the powers within?

And, yes, I am racked by the question: WHY DID I NOT TELL HER ABOUT MY RESEARCH??

I could have leaped up and announced that I, Karai, know about these so-called markers. That after seeing her research, I became interested in the mystical secrets of blood. That I, too, have tinkered with the very fabric that makes people who they are. Connecting these markers to the Loculi, as Mother has done—this is genius indeed. But consider, Diary, what my own paltry scientific ability has achieved![10] It has led to my proudest achievement—altering

---

10 Admittedly along with hours and hours spent with wizards and alchemists sworn to secrecy.

the markers themselves. You remember, I began first with a few creatures such as Kav'i the vizzeet. At first I wanted to create super-beings—men and women who could fly of their own accord and such things. But humans have physical limits. So I sought to change the natural abilities of a living, breathing human being. To *magnify* a particular talent that he or she already possesses. To stretch the untapped regions of the brain itself!

Most exciting, Diary, I believe each such altered person will be able to pass this trait onward, so that not only Atlanteans but their children and their children's children will have these special abilities!

Why is this not equal to Mother's achievement? Well, it is. Although absolute proof of this last part will have to wait. I will meet Mother tomorrow and learn about the mysterious Loculi. And in the meantime I will let Massarym bask in his excitement. But I will hope that he heals promptly. News has just arrived that he landed badly from a Loculus flight and twisted his ankle.

Ah, well.

The Great Onyx Circle, Thursday afternoon

I COULD NOT rouse Massarym early enough to accompany Mother to the Great Onyx Circle. So I agreed we would meet her as soon as we could. Accompanied by Father, we set out in the late morning. Diary, it has been such a long time since my last visit that I'd nearly forgotten the booby traps constructed by my ancestors to protect the mazelike pathways. Some of them are downright lethal. But I brought along crazy old Kav'i to help us through. Largely this was because my experiment had given him extraordinary navigational powers. But it was also to impress and baffle my brother.

I had also forgotten what a foul, dark, godsforsaken, cramped path of sweat-soaked soil leads through the trees into the center of the ridged circle. The ground is so rutted and pocked with animal holes that it's a miracle I didn't break my ankle.

It was not surprising that an impulsive, monkeylike creature of small intellect would bound heedlessly ahead of me in the maze. But I didn't expect Kav'i to do the same.[11]

It wasn't until Kav'i sneezed in Massarym's direction that I realized I'd forgotten to tell my brother a crucial detail. Unfortunately, a side effect of my experiment with Kav'i had imbued this generation of vizzeets with acidic, acrid spittle.

"*Don't let s–s–spit make contact with your skin!*" I shouted, racing toward my brother.

"GEEEEAAAAAHHH!" Massarym bellowed in pain. "Now you tell me!" He was jumping up and down in agony. "That . . . *thing* sneezed on my leg! What on earth did he eat for breakfast—scorpion venom?"

---

11 HA!! Yes, I am wicked, but only in private.

Kav'i was crouched guiltily at the base of the tunnel wall, all elbows and knees. "Little Kav'itaki, I asked y-y-y-you never to spit on me, you scamp!" I said.

"*You?* What about *me?*" Massarym burst into sudden motion, swinging for the back of my head. I ducked, but not quite fast enough, and his arm caught me lightly on the ear. Kav'i began screeching and bouncing up and down, eyes rolling in his head, pounding his tiny fists on the rock floor.

Our commotion brought back Father, who had walked on ahead. He grabbed each of us by the wrist and stepped between us. "Careful, boys! That insane monkey doesn't know you're playing around. You're just winding it up. Behave."

"Uh, that monster just sneezed a layer of skin off my thigh," Massarym said. "Maybe we should release him into the wild."

"Without him, it w-w-would take us t-t—"

"Out with it, my son," Father said. "You are among family who love you."

Diary, when will he know my slippery tongue has nothing to do with that?

"*Twice* as long to find our way through the m-m-maze," I pointed out. "When was . . . last time you came out here—three, four years ago? I can't remember the path at all. That insane monkey . . . he r-r-remembers it all."

"You slugabeds could have woken up early with your mother, who also knows the way, and then we'd be spared the company of a dangerous little vizzeet with questionable sanity," Father said, eyebrows raised. "But it is advantageous to have him, considering your mother is the only one of us familiar with the correct path these days."

"So . . . you knew about her p-p-project, too, Father?" I said. "About the Loculi?"

"Well, yes," Father said.

"And you never s-said a thing?" I pressed on.

Father tugged on the end of his beard. "As the king consort it usually serves me well to not let on how much I know, for various reasons relating to matters of state."

"I knew, too!" Massarym said with a grin.

"That is obvious, after the public sh-show you put on, Mass," I said.

"Speaking of public shows, Karai, since when have you been studying Akkadian?" Father asked. "Your mother was very upset. She confided that she believed—"

"She believed I s-stole a L-Loculus!" I said. "But she doesn't anymore. I told her."

Father shrugged. "Well, you may need to work on her a bit more . . ."

I could not believe my ears. After our talk, she *still* thought I was lying!

"No human being can learn languages that quickly,"

Massarym said with a mocking grin. "Especially one who can barely speak Atlantean. You should learn to rely on the truth more often, Brother."

Diary, I can keep my temper for an admirable time, as you know. But when I am pushed to the wall, I push back. "The t-truth?" I blurted out. "The truth is that I've been conducting my own exp-p-periments! While you've been eating g-g-g—"

"Grapes?" Massarym said. "I love grapes."

"—And taking long ch-ch-ch-chariot rides, I have been t-training with wizards, learning the s-secrets of nature. In fact, I've used science to give myself the ability to p-pick up languages just by listening!" I couldn't help smiling with pride.

"Very good little speech," Massarym said. "Perhaps you won't stutter when you speak Ak-k-kadian! So tell me, are these the same experiments that made this vizzeet into an acid-spitting little monster?"

"Well, yes." My smile faded, remembering how my experiments had also transformed the vromaski . . . and the griffin . . . but that could wait. "But only by exp-perimenting on animals could I refine my t-t-t—"

"Taste? Tongue-twisting ability?" Massarym asked. "Oh, no, wait—*technique*! It must not be that refined, if you can't cure your own speech issues."

Enough.

"You're r-r-right—in fact, my spit burns like Kav'i's!" I said, hocking a big wad of phlegm. As I pantomimed spitting it at Massarym, he hopped away with a very unprincely "Eeeew!"

Father sighed. "Can we continue? It is rather . . . *close* in these woods."

We walked onward, letting Kav'i go on a safe distance ahead. Soon the smell of sulfur began to waft toward us as we neared the center of the circular ridge. "Pee-ew," Massarym said with great maturity. "Sorry, everyone, guess I shouldn't have had figs for breakfast."

No one but Massarym laughed.

As we entered the clearing at the center of the Great Onyx Circle, I glanced around at the ridge. Once overgrown with trees, it was sparser now. The ridge itself had indeed begun to rise, for reasons completely unknown. Uprooted pines lay in chaotic brown piles, some having rolled to the bottom of the slope. To our right was the great Atlantean waterfall, fed by the magic spring. Higher than I'd ever seen it, the cascade of falling water thundered into a pool underneath. Diary, this spring feeds many rivulets and underground waterways, a network of magical water flowing deep into the land itself.

Mother was walking toward us now, out of the watery mist. "Come," she commanded, turning away.

"Good to see you, too," Massarym said, flinching away

as Father raised a threatening hand.

Mother led us across the vast, flat center of the Great Onyx Circle. In the distance I could see the glowing mists of the rift.

As boys, Massarym and I had attempted to sneak into this place. Time and again, we were defeated by the complexity of the maze—or the scoldings of the great priests, who always managed to appear out of nowhere as if spawned by the trees.

Now nothing was stopping us. Soon I could see that the rift was no longer a mere crack in the earth, wreathed in thick vapors. First, the hilt of a golden sword jutted from its center. Second, a circle of carved marble had been constructed around the rift. Within that circle were seven smaller hemispherical depressions, each filled with a clear, glowing orb. And inside each orb was neither liquid nor gas, but a tangle of shifting shapes that seemed to flow freely from sphere to sphere, changing colors and intensities by the moment. Each had a translucent, filigreed casing, as if someone had drizzled molten silver over the lot. The whole construction looked like a shrine to a god I had never heard of.

"Welcome to the Heptakiklos, the Circle of Seven," Mother said with a broad smile. I sensed a lecture coming on.[12] "This rift energy is why our people are healthier,

---

12 Forgive me for re-creating the lecture here AGAIN, Diary. But this time, there is good reason. Trust me.

stronger, and live longer and more productive lives than people anywhere else in the world. Our scientists and philosophers are centuries ahead of even the best in the Greek academies. Even our plants are healthier. Why? It's not because we work harder or because we're more disciplined or because we have good bloodlines. It's because of *this*." She reached out her hands, cupped in a bowl, scooped up a handful of mist, and let it flow through her fingers.

Massarym puffed up his cheeks and blew on it. "It changes colors."[13]

"This mist—what we call Telion—has elemental power," Mother continued. "It infuses the water of the spring, and a small amount flows into the very groundwater underneath every Atlantean's feet. While we of the royal family come here, directly to the source, for our healing and restoration, every single one of our citizens partakes of this water without even realizing it."

My brain was bursting with questions. Of course we knew about the Telion and the rift . . . but these Loculi were simply astounding. I could tell which was which, but for the Loculus of Invisibility. It was a perfect sphere of swirling colorful gas with no membrane discernible to the eye.

"As energy emerges from the rift," Mother said, "much of it is captured by the Heptakiklos, where it passes from

13 Oh dear gods, Diary, is it possible he was switched at birth?

31

Loculus to Loculus. What you see now is perfect equilibrium—all seven Loculi together in balance, mere vessels for the awesome magic. Ah, but once a Loculus is removed, it all changes. The removed Loculus instantly takes on one specific component of the Telion—just one set of particular properties. The Loculus of Invisibility disappears. The Loculus of Flight—well, you get the idea. These are all properties with a purpose—to give the bearer magical qualities so he or she can better protect the Loculi!"

"But . . . what about the b-balance?" I said. "If one Loculus is removed, what happens to the Atlantean energy?"

"It becomes like a many-headed hydra that has lost one of its heads," Father said with a chuckle. "It must compensate. The other Loculi, I suppose, absorb the extra energy."

"And there is no p-price to pay for this instability?" I said. "For stealing away two Loculi to impress foreign visitors?"

Massarym yawned. "Envy is so unbecoming in a future king."

"There are many things we do not know." Mother spoke up. "But, my beloved family, I have labored long and hard on this. These Loculi exist to protect our future. We will be able to—"

Massarym burped. Eyes glued to the shimmering orbs, he was fidgeting in his place, rocking back and forth on the balls of his feet, not listening to a word Mother was saying.

"Massarym!" she snapped.

He blinked as if just discovering she was in the room. "Oh. Yes. Bravo, Mother."

"May I ask a question?" I said, ignoring my brother. "Why not l-l-leave the rift alone? Have we ever needed these Loculi?"

"They're fun," Massarym piped up.

"In a world of perfect harmony, we would not need Loculi," Mother said. "A world in which nations support other nations, live side by side, and leave well enough alone. Having the sea on all sides has protected us from invasion, from snooping. But now men have learned to navigate and build better ships, and water is no longer a barrier. This means we are now vulnerable."

"From whom?" I asked. I had never seen any fighting, only read stories of the great wars in Athens and Egypt. "Nobody has ever made an at-t-ttempt at our sea walls."

"Under cover of night, our guards have fended off some rather weak attacks." Mother waved her hand as if to banish our fears, carving a path through the thick mist. It eddied in swirls, then filled in that path like water. "Barbarians. Gauls. Celts. Small raiding parties. Nothing we couldn't handle."

"M-M-Mass, did *you* know about this?" I said.

Massarym raised his eyebrows and shrugged. "N-N-Nope."

I drew my hand to smack him, and he darted away.

Father's mouth was set in a hard line, staring out over

Mother's shoulder. "Nor I," he said dryly.

"Not Father either?" I blurted out. "Have you a secret army? Why didn't you tell us? Are we not also p-p-protectors of this nation? Shouldn't I know these things if one day I'm going to be k-k—" I stopped myself and looked over at Massarym. He doesn't love to be reminded that he's second in line to the throne.

"I thought it best to keep these small diversions to myself and the army, to avoid undue panic," Mother said. "My own energies have been consumed with my science—with developing the Loculi. Your father—well, he has a different idea. He believes he can use the Loculus of Strength to defend the country if necessary. A rather doomed strategy, I would think—one man against legions. Which is why I kept news of these attacks from him too."

She gave Father a withering look. He coughed, looked away, and did not answer. The distant thunder of the waterfall echoed throughout in the great bowl created by the ridge.

"If more attempts are made on our borders you will all be notified," Mother continued. "But these Loculi are designed to ensure that this will not happen. Why do you think the Akkadians traveled all the way from Mesopotamia to meet us, a journey that surely took months?"

"Arishti-Aya heard of my smoldering good looks," Massarym said.

Mother's grave expression broke into a smile. "Perhaps. But equally likely is that our land has become legend. Scholars write of us, and Atlanteans who have made the crossing to the mainland are treated like geniuses and celebrities. They call our Telion the 'Atlantean Force.' The Akkadians certainly were hoping to discover something of our secret when they came calling. And we allowed them to, did we not?"

"We did," Massarym said.

"*You* did," I retorted.

"Dear Qalani," Father interrupted. "No disrespect intended, but is revealing our secret the wisest choice? Why not keep the Telion a bit of a mystery? Why even let these rather festive little spheres out of this hiding place?"

"Father's right," I said. "You have c-created something that can be s-stolen, Mother! A land with a big-enough army can raid these things and take them for their own—"

"They can't, because they don't have our royal blood!" Massarym said.

"Wh-which gives them a reason to t-try to take our blood, too!" I said.

My words hung in the sulphuric air. No one had thought of this.

"Karai, please . . ." Mother said, her lip curled with disgust.

"Nonsense, Karai—if we are attacked or taken over, we will fly away—*fffft!*—and take these powers with us," Massarym said, knifing his hand through the mist like a bird taking off. "Atlantis can be reborn anywhere, O Future King. Or would you prefer that we were paupers in a distant land, eating mice and forever insisting we were royalty in a past life?"

"If we were attacked, you would be the first to run away," I said.

"Oh?" Massarym replied, puffing out his chest. "Try me."

"Boys . . ." Mother said with a warning tone.

We all stood there in silence for a moment. As always, Diary, I had so much more to say, but I felt tongue-tied. What Mother and Massarym had said made a certain sense, but I couldn't stop myself from feeling it was all wrong.

That the Loculi, by their very existence, were dangerous.

That capturing the Telion, rather than allowing it to flow as nature intended, was harmful.

That separating the Loculi, for any reason, was a disruption in the strength and integration of the energy.

That this disruption could weaken this glorious gift that the earth has given us.

But did I say these things, Diary? You know me well. OF COURSE NOT.

All that came out of my well-educated mouth was, "I don't know. I just don't know."

Brilliant.

"You are rightfully concerned, Karai," Mother said. "The Telion has massive power and comes from the very center of the earth. And we do not understand everything about it. So we must take precautions." She aimed a frown at Massarym. "No borrowing the Loculi for party games, understood?"

Massarym scowled.

Mother slipped her hand into Father's, and I could see the tension ebb from his face. "And as for your father's excellent point about theft, this leads to my next request." She snapped her focus to me. "The ridge creates an extraordinary echo, Karai. I heard your little confession regarding your . . . experiments."

"I—I—" My face was heating up.

"Do not be embarrassed, I suspected as much," Mother said. "How else could you have you accomplished your feat with the Akkadians? Very impressive, too, that you have altered the characteristics of vizzeets and vromaskis. But playing games with the blood of human life can be extremely dangerous."

I opened my mouth to protest, but she placed her index finger over it gently.

"However," she said, "at the moment I think we *need*

something extremely dangerous—to protect the Loculi. A creature, perhaps. One that on its own is fearsome . . . but perhaps could be made unstoppable. A fierce, predatory creature . . ."

These words were like music to me. I felt a grin stretch across my face. "Like maybe . . . a g-g-griffin?"

Massarym arched his eyebrows, his dark eyes wide as moonfruit. "Oh dear gods, playing with griffins?" he said. "Big brother will never survive."

"Oh?" I replied. "Try me."

Thursday afternoon

DIARY, AM I crazy?

I thought we left the Great Onyx Circle with an agreement. I concluded we would proceed lightly with the Loculi. We would not remove them from the Heptakiklos for frivolous reasons.

Mother, it turns out, had concluded something different.

She thought it would be a lovely idea to say good-bye to the Akkadians with another exhibition at the Parade Grounds—this one with *all* the Loculi. "Not only for the Akkadians," she said, "but also for our own people." Putting all the cards on the table, she said, would impress, delight, and inspire.

While I stood there spluttering and spitting like a teapot,

she told me my hair had grown long and shaggy in the last few months while I've been preoccupied in the laboratory. So in preparation for the display, I was forced to wait in my chambers for Aram, the barber.

It is at times like these that I wish I_were king. I would make sure that everyone's actions *made sense*. And no one would ever need a haircut.

Aram's hair is even bushier and more unkempt than mine, but he's a wizard with the scissors. He also likes to talk.

"What's wrong?" he asked, raising one of his bushy black eyebrows as he placed a protective cape over my tunic.

"Sorry, j-j-just haven't had t-t-time—" I began.

"No, not that. You're scratching your neck like a dog."

"I am?" I said.

"Ugh, I need to check you for lice, don't I?" Aram rolled up his sleeves, pulled a pair of gloves from his pack, grabbed my shoulders, and wrenched my neck to one side. "I don't care how your hair looks, Your Highness, but if you're going to let it get like this and not keep it clean, this kind of thing is bound to happen. How long has it been itching?"

Was I scratching? Honestly, I hadn't really noticed—but, yes, now that he had mentioned it[14] . . . "A few weeks,

---

14 Diary, YOU never lie. Reading back over the previous entries, I do see ample evidence of this! Scratch, scratch, scratch, scratch . . . like a mangy dog! What did Atlanteans think of their future King Karai the Canine?

I guess . . ." I began. "Right after I—"

Right after I subjected myself to my own experiments.

I considered telling the truth but thought better of confiding in Aram the Blabbermouth. "R-right after I spent time with the a-an—"

"Animal trainers, of course," Aram said with a knowing nod. "Must be lice."

His fingers picked through my hair, lifting it off my scalp. His shears began to snip away, and chunks of blond fluff fell by my feet. Aram muttered to himself as he worked. "Hmm, this is interesting. No creepy crawlies that I can see. Dry scalp, maybe."

It felt good to lose the hair. My head felt lighter. All of a sudden Aram's hands stopped, holding my hair up and away from the back of my head. "Well, by the griffin's gizzards, would you look at this."

He handed me a small mirror. Looking into it, I saw the higgledy-piggledy thatch of half-cut hair, as if a vizzeet had cut it with scissors dipped in spit. "Um, Aram, I look like a human haystack. Maybe keep going?"

"Just look here." He grabbed the handle of the mirror and angled it so I could see behind my head, where he was holding another mirror.

In the center of a cleanly cut area at the rear of my skull, my hair was strangely discolored. There were two distinct white streaks, starting near the base of my head and meeting in a point at the top.

It looked like this: Λ

"Odd," Aram said, tossing the mirror to the side and resuming my haircut.

Odd, yes, Diary. But it sent a chill down my spine.

Here I must confess to you one memorable moment during a research session:

I imagined, during the wee hours that morning, a new future filled with those who would benefit from my work. I saw young people developing powers from the very talents they were born with. Astonishing powers. But in this age of ocean travel and potential conquest, I fretted that they would scatter around the world. Soon generations would not know one another, lost to their origins, far from the Atlantean shores. Could they ever learn about each other? How would they unite?

This was deeply on my mind, as the potions roiled and the exact titrations continued. It was all I could think about until a flash of consuming light blinded me and threw me to the wall. In a moment I felt as if the experiment were both inside and outside me at the same time. I saw tiny flecks of matter swimming, rearranging into new forms. As my mind cleared, I found myself on the floor.

Exhausted and exhilarated, I fell asleep right there. As I drifted off, I pictured these lost young people again—but now in my dream they were discovering that they were not alone. I saw a leader. I saw followers. They rose, soaring above the mundane world on their own plane of existence. They were in formation, like a flock of majestic birds! The image was clear as day in this magnificent dream.

Thursday evening

THE SUN IS high with barely a cloud in the sky. The stands are full of people; the weather is perfect for a sporting event. Today is not merely for invited guests. All Atlantis has been asked to come, and people occupy every seat, every entrance, and the tops of every fence. As you know, Diary, I've never been comfortable in the role of entertainer. It has always been much easier to sit in the royal booth and watch hulking athletes compete. So here I am, scribbling in this journal in the tunnels underneath the Parade Grounds, with the Loculus of Flight in a pack at my feet.

I haven't tried it yet. I'm a little bit nervous. But Mother, sensing my envy of Massarym, has granted me the opportunity. "I have been thinking," she told me, "and I agree with you that the people should see their future king in a position of strength. On this occasion, you shall demonstrate the Loculus."

Given the circumstances, I could not say no. But I would so rather be in my lab or reading a book. What if I fall?

Diary, I am impossibly nervous.

On the other hand, it *is* flying! How bad can it be?

Massarym is here with me in the corridor. He, of course, upon hearing of Mother's decision, insisted upon having a role in the demonstration, which now will include several of the Loculi. I am appalled by this, Diary. I believe that removing so many Loculi will have an effect on the Telion, but no one seems to share my concern.

Ah well. The sun is spilling down through the archway. I can hear the crowd. IF MASSARYM LOOKS OVER MY SHOULDER, I WILL USE SECRET SCIENCE TO GIVE HIM THREE NOSES.

By the sun god Helios, Karai smells three times worse than ever!!

My Diary, sullied and greased by the hand of boorish Massarym! Do not catch fire or disintegrate, Diary, I need you!

Later Thursday evening

IT IS FINISHED.

Thank you for being here, Diary, to record this day.

My hands are still shaking. I have to admit, it was a bit of fun. Massarym insisted I was lucky to be the one who got the Loculus of Flight. I had convinced myself I would lose control and be dashed upon the rocks, leaving Massarym to be king. "You," I told him gloomily, "are the lucky one!"

Once I finally steeled my courage (and my bladder), I ducked out of the tunnel onto the grassy expanse of the Parade Ground.

And I froze.

The whole stadium seemed to spin—people everywhere I looked. The noise of the crowd boxed my ears. But it wasn't all cheers. Soldiers stood guard around the perimeter of the oval grounds. On one side a young man struggled against two of them, shouting something I couldn't quite understand. In seconds he was gone.

What was the cause of this? I could not imagine.

"Anybody home?" Massarym shouted above the din.

This shocked me back to the task at hand. The Loculus was out of my pack and in my grip. Who had done this? Had I taken it out? I don't remember. But my feet left the ground and I was hovering in the air, as high as Massarym's shoulders. The roar of the crowd was deafening. I nearly lost my balance and the roar turned to a shocked "Ooooh!"

I fought off panic and allowed myself to rise upward. It was as if the orb were responding to my thoughts, acting as an extension of my brain! Before I could even think the word *left*, I was zipping to the left. I tried to relax and let myself connect to the Loculus. I shot up into the sky, looped upside down—and then zoomed back to the ground, landing on my feet.

Diary, I never dreamed I would be writing this, but—it was easy! Yes, you heard that right.

Massarym[15] was hoisting a gigantic boulder over his head using the Loculus of Strength, while simultaneously using the Loculus of Invisibility to disappear, making it look like the boulder was levitating all by itself.

Ha! I took the chance to launch straight up into the blue, cloudless sky.

The crowd, my family, the noise—everything shrank and fell away. The strong wind in the sky whipped in my ears as I glanced down at the Parade Grounds. The stadium was a tiny platter on a green table; my family looked like ants. I wobbled as the ground swam before my eyes. Quickly I looked away from the ground, toward the top of the Great Onyx Circle.

Despite the clear day, the top of the circular ridge was ringed with dark clouds. Lightning knifed from the sky down onto the peak. Curtains of rain darkened the trees. It was as if the entire area was in a different day . . . or a different world.

I looked back down at the performance below me, then again at the Great Onyx Circle.

Something was definitely wrong.

Karai! came a call, distant but directly in my ear.

Karai!

---

15 Please forgive the mention of He Who Spoilt the Sanctity of Thy Pages.

I hovered in the air, staring at the roiling mess in the sky above the Circle and suddenly I realized it was Massarym's voice I was hearing. *Come back down*, it said. *Karai!*

This is what I mean, Diary, when I say twins have a special connection. They can communicate without speaking—even twins who are as different from each other as Massarym and I are.

Then I felt a hand on my shoulder. I would have jumped in shock, but you can't really jump when you're hovering in the sky.

I whipped my head around. There was Massarym, floating beside me. A mile up in the air.

"H-how—" I spluttered.

"YEEEOWW!" Massarym held tightly to my shoulder. Another Loculus was in his free hand. "This one is . . . remarkable," he said through gritted teeth. "It instantly transports you to wherever you want to go—*zzzzap*! Mother calls it teleportation. Not as fun as the others. It hurts to use it."

"Incredible!" I said.

"I think I'll call it the Loculus of Zap," he said. "Painful but spectacular."

"Massarym, you know s-s-something odd?" I said. "You are holding on to me, yet I do not feel your w-weight."

"Really . . . AAAAAAHHH!" As an experiment, he had let go. And now he was plummeting downward!

I could see him fumbling with his Loculus of Zap, but in his panic he let go, sending the orb off into the air.

Get him.

My Loculus responded, accelerating me downward at a speed faster than Massarym's. As I touched his shoulder, my brother's fall ceased.

I wrapped my arm around his waist. He was again flying with me. Together we continued onward to the falling Loculus, and Massarym plucked that safely from the air.

"Th-th-thank you!" Massarym stammered. "By the gods, I sound like you!"

"Ha ha!" I bellowed with joy. "Massarym, we now understand a p-property of the Loculi! The power to fly transferred from me to you, when I t-touched you!"

Massarym gulped. I could see the thoughts bouncing around in his head. "So perhaps we can also use the Loculus of Zap to return instantly—"

But my attention was drawn to a frightening sight not far away—an angry thicket of black clouds gathering over the Great Onyx Circle. "Massarym, look what's going on over the r-ridge!" I said.

I extended my arm to point, and Massarym lost his grip again. As he plummeted back toward the ground, I steered the Loculus of Flight into a dive after him, willing it to move me faster, reaching with my free hand as I gained on him. He hadn't gone far. I had improved my skill.

Then he disappeared.

I kept diving, right through the empty space where he had been.

The Parade Grounds grew nearer—Mother, Father, the Loculi scattered on the ground around them. Mother was shouting Massarym's name. The crowd was hushed and agape. Massarym reappeared inches above the ground, then crashed down on top of one of the Loculi lying around Mother and Father's feet. I saw his eyes widen as he realized that even though the teleportation had worked—he had gone from the air to the ground—it hadn't stopped his momentum. He hit the ground with the same force he had been falling.

The crowd gasped. Some fainted. Massarym lay on the ground, crumpled like a piece of parchment, his back arched into an impossible curve over the Loculus he'd landed on.

Mother covered her mouth and ran to him. I touched down, dropped the Loculus of Flight, and knelt beside my brother.

A shocked murmur swept through the crowd. Massarym wasn't moving.

"Oh, no. Oh, no!" Mother moaned. She turned her eyes to me, full of tears. "What were you thinking?"

I said nothing. The last few moments of Massarym's life played themselves in my head over and over—the black clouds above the Great Onyx Circle, Massarym's voice in my ear. My hand, pointing to the ridge. Why did not my

48

brother's safety take priority over the weather? What *was* I thinking?

Massarym's body was convulsing. But now one leg, twisted horrifically underneath him, straightened. He coughed again. His arm, hanging limply to his side, popped back into joint.

He grimaced as his body realigned itself. His legs bent back into their normal shape and he rolled to his side, off the glowing blue Loculus onto which he'd landed. "Well, that was fun," he said, "in an extremely painful way."

The crowd roared, rising to their feet

At the sight of Massarym's sudden resurrection, Father stood and let out a loud roar of relief, shock, and happiness. I thought Mother would do the same, but her face darkened. "You did that on purpose, Massarym, did you not?"

"Would I do something like that, Mother?" Massarym said, grinning sheepishly.

"Something like what?" Father said.

"He fell," Mother said, "on the Loculus of Healing. He planned this."

Massarym pushed himself to a standing position. "All right, all right. Hey, I knew it would work. Right? Our Loculi never fail."

Smiling, he waved to the crowd.

And they went wild.

* * *

As I write this now, just before retiring to sleep, I cannot help but report that the sunset was beautiful. Why mention this, you may ask, Diary? Because I was able to see it above the silhouette of the Great Onyx Circle.

Yes, shortly after the Loculi were returned, there was no sign of the horrible storm that had been there hours before.

Friday

COUSIN NELIK CAME by the lab today. He's been helping me out for the last few months. His parents dote on him, Diary. Nearly every day Lady Karissa and Lord Al'duin report to Mother that Nelik is a genius at mathematics. He is good, it's true, even though he's only thirteen years old, almost four years younger than I am. And I like working with him.

But I wonder exactly how Mother and Father describe me to others? A genius? I hope so. But I think not.

If I were to describe him, *chatterbox* would be the first word that came to mind.

"Karai, those magic orbs your mother invented are AMAZING!" Nelik said as he banged the door open. "Will you teach me how to use them? I want to fly! And lift huge rocks! And go invisible! Do you think we could figure out how she made them? Maybe we could make a set for me!"

"Nelik, I have n-n-no idea how she made them. I'm

not even sure she knows herself," I said. "Plus, you can't y-y-y . . . use them."

His face fell. "Why not?"

"They are off-limits to anyone but the royal f-f-family," I said.

"I'm your cousin! I am part of the royal family!" Nelik protested.

"*Immediate* royal family, n-n-not extended royal family," I had to tell him.

"But I'm still alive!" he said.

I had to think about that for a moment. "*Extended*, not *expended*," I said. "And it doesn't m-m-m-matter whether they work or not on you—they are off-limits. End of discussion."

This, of course, only made things worse. Nelik looked as though I'd slapped him. "Well," he said, turning to leave, "I thought we were friends."

"We are!" I exclaimed.

He reached for the doorknob.

"Hey!" I called. "Hey, hey. I've got something else really c-c-cool that you *can* try. Remember what we did with the vizzeets, when we gave them the serum that changed their b-blood?"

"Oh, fun, you're going to make me spit like a vizzeet . . ." Nelik sniffed.

"No!" I said quickly. "I've refined the p-p-p-process. The blood can be altered in many different ways—wonderful ways! I'm sure it's safe on humans—well, because I've tried it on m-myself."

He turned around warily. "What kind of wonderful ways?"

"Guess who can speak Akkadian?" I grinned at him. "With no st-stammering?

"Just like that—change the blood, know a language?" Nelik asked. "That makes no sense."

"It's the abi-ab-ability to *learn* languages," I said. "You lock it in—vocabulary, structure, all of it—each time you hear a c-conversation."

"Children can do that," Nelik said with a shrug.

"Not like this," I insisted. "Not this f-fast."

He looked decidedly unimpressed. "I want to be able to zoom around in the air like Massarym."

Like Massarym. I couldn't believe my ears. Not Nelik, too!

"By the gods, Nelik," I groaned, "please give me just a few hours when I don't have to think about my stupid b-brother!"

"Oooh, princes aren't supposed to say *stupid*," Nelik said gleefully.

Yes, Diary, that was uncalled-for. Yes, I am sometimes less mature than my impetuous cousin.

"I'm s-sorry," I said. "But think about this, my cousin— changing the blood holds so much more p-p-potential than depending on some orb. You love sports, yes? What if I can make you run f-faster, jump higher, never get tired—without a Loculus?"

He looked intrigued.

"I know the exact ingredient in your blood that limits your per . . . performance," I told him. "I can t-target it and get rid of it. By tonight, you'll be su . . . superhuman. And if my theory is correct, your ch-children will also have your new abilities."

"Children?" Nelik looked aghast. "I don't have children!"

"In the future!" I said.

"In that case," he said. "Yes. Make me superhuman. Prove it."

I felt a moment's unease, thinking about what my mother had said about playing games with heredity. But then I thought, *I tried it on myself and I'm fine. She's just envious of what I might accomplish.*

"Let's get ready," I said, gathering the supplies I needed.

Saturday

THIS MORNING MOTHER, Father, and I introduced the griffin to the Heptakiklos. We set a vromaski loose with the instructions to fetch a Loculus.

I pitied what happened to the vromaski.

Though the sight was disgusting, Mother and Father

both praised the work I had done. The transformation of the griffin from a predator of small animals to an instrument of killing.

I summoned up the courage to ask Mother about the clouds I had seen over the Great Onyx Circle, but she dismissed my concerns. "Once we returned the Loculi, those indeed vanished," she said. "We will be sure to take precautions not to remove them."

And that was that.

But, Diary, there's been something else brewing besides the storms above the ridge and Nelik's new blood.

Arishti-Aya.

No, *she's* not brewing, Diary. I am writing about my affections for her.[16]

First I was just talking to her to practice my Akkadian, but now it's because she's funny and smart. And I really like staring into her huge, almond-shaped eyes.

Today, on the final day of the Akkadian visit, she told me I can call her Aya.

I summoned her this morning to the Royal Garden to have one last word, with Massarym nowhere in sight to hog her attention.[17]

---

16 In case the Evil Massarym is sneaking a look at this, all I have to say is, stick your fat face in a rotten pomegranate.

17 Because everywhere she is, Massarym the Massively Annoying pops out of nowhere, goofing around, trying to make her laugh. Which she does, just to humor him. It's *really* nauseating.

My Akkadian is now near fluent. Every sentence I hear is like a complete lesson. I find myself recognizing words I had no knowledge of until moments earlier. I told her—vaguely—of my experiments, and she was rapt. Aya's laugh, musical and fluttery, is a priceless reward. I've been trying to teach her a little bit of Atlantean, and she's doing remarkably well.

"I wish I could learn like you do," she said.

"Ah, but you are doing so well!" I replied, scratching the back of my head.

Karai, listen to yourself, a voice screamed in my head—*speaking Akkadian with no stammer, with no difficulty whatever!*

"But could you zap me with your special science *uddu-uddu*?"[18] Aya said with a laugh. "Whatever it is . . ."

"A field of energy, brought about by magical elixirs I have been developing with wizards from the palace, that rebuilds the structure of the blood so that its flow to the brain actually rebuilds its architecture in such a way that—" Her eyes were glazing over, so I stopped. "I'm sorry. It's all I can think about sometimes."

"*All* you can think of?" Aya said, a tiny smile growing across her face.

Oh, Diary. Oh, dear Diary. If you could but feel a

---

18 *Uddu-uddu*—meaning *what do you call it*, more or less. It's a great word to know.

fraction of the excitement coursing through me in that moment, your pages would explode, scattering to the four winds.

"Well . . ." I began.

"Will you think of me when I'm gone, Karai?" she said. "I wish we were staying longer. Maybe one day we'll come back. Or you could sneak away on one of those round . . . *uddu-uddu* things your brother loves to play with. You could fly over to our kingdom and come visit me."

I felt my cheeks flush. She smiled and looked away. What was I supposed to say? Talking to girls is Massarym's specialty. He would have pushed his dark hair away from his face and smiled in that way that just makes girls laugh immediately. He would have said *Sure! When should I come over?* just like that. He becomes relaxed and confident, I become scared.

Maybe someday I will be able to fix this through science— instead of doing what I did at that moment, which was . . . *talk about science!*

(Yes, Diary, I am a fool.)

"I probably shouldn't tell you this, but Mother is afraid of foreign powers trying to take Atlantis over," I blathered, "so the Loculi are almost a way of saving up, or concentrating, the Atlantean Force in such a way that if something happens we can just—" I flew my hand through the air like a bird.

She looked alarmed. "So then why would you show them off to my father and his men? Our country would benefit from these . . . Lobuli . . . so they *would* pose a temptation."

"But your father is a good—"

"A good king, yes," Aya said. "But there have been problems with courtiers and also with unrest among the people. There is no telling what would happen if word gets out. Dear Karai, your continent has been a place of harmony and trust, but the rest of the world . . ."

I wanted nothing more than to soothe her worries. "They only work for . . . *some* people, Aya, not all," I said. "Plus we keep them hidden in a place that only we know how to reach. And they are now guarded by unbeatable foes—griffins!"

"Grif-fin?" she said, sounding the word out.

"It looks like a lion, but with an eagle's head and neck. And wings," I explained. "Usually they live high in the mountaintops, hunting small game and laying eggs. They are peaceful and lazy—except when they sense a threat on their young. I have seen how they were able to use their natural defenses in an aggressive way, and so I . . . er, trained them to protect the Loculi as they would their babies. Anyone who came close would be torn to shreds."

"This all makes sense, but defending your Loculi is not what worries me." Aya turned toward me, looking at my eyes, then at my feet. "It's your own people, dear Karai.

Your wild exhibition was impressive, but it was also very, very frightening. Your family has power so far beyond what any other human being has ever had . . ." She hesitated before going on. "Showing that off can delight people for a moment but create mistrust and resentment forever."

I didn't answer. My brain raced to keep up with the stream of foreign language, picking up mostly everything.

"My father came to Atlantis to see how you managed to keep peaceful rule for so many hundreds of years," Aya added. "But as we walked through the city that night, much of the talk our translator heard was rebellious and resentful. Some people see you as gods. Others want the power you have. And they believe they have reason to fear you."

Fear us? Diary, these words landed on my ears like a hammer.

"But—the people know we wouldn't use our powers to harm them," I said.

"Really?" she said, her eyes moistening. "Karai, this scares me. What if one of your own people tries to steal the Loculi? Would the griffin murder one of your own citizens?"

"You—you really care about this," I said. It was the first time I had slipped into a stammer in Akkadian.

"How would it feel to have your own people's blood on your hands?" she said. "Your citizens have been happy for so long. Wouldn't you be safest to keep it that way?"

She's shrewd, smart, and knows about governing. She was speaking wisely about danger from within. I knew I should be concerned, Diary. But at the moment all I could think about was her as Atlantean queen, by my side. She, not I, would be running the operations of the country, while I worked on my science.

I didn't say any of this, of course. In fact, before I could say anything at all, my tunic was pulled up over my head. Something shoved me hard from behind. I stumbled forward—right into Aya's arms, like a forceful, thoughtless brute!

I quickly stepped away and yanked my tunic back, feeling as though not just my face but my entire head was on fire. Aya was biting her lip to stop from laughing.

"Awww, she wants to give you a hug, Karai!" Massarym's voice floated out of nowhere.

"She can't understand you, you fool!" I shouted in Atlantean.

"Tell her what I said!" I began to feel my brother's fingers poking my ribs all around. I bent out of the way and flailed blindly at the air around me. *"Massarym!"* I shouted. Aya jumped to avoid me, then lost her footing and began to fall. I reached out to grab her arm, keep her up, and all of a sudden we were in a heap on the ground.

I jerked my head up and away from hers, conscious of her breath brushing my cheek. As I leaped up, Massarym appeared out of nowhere, arms folded, grinning. Something heavy thumped to the ground—the Loculus of Invisibility, no doubt. I whirled and shoved him, hard, in the chest. He staggered back, the smile on his face unchanged.

"Leave . . . me . . . alone!" I grunted. I was off-balance, furious. I couldn't see past my own fists, and I aimed a fist at my brother's chest.

Massarym whirled out of the way and calmly bent to offer a hand to Aya. "Please, miss, let me help you. My brother doesn't know his own strength." She took his hand and stood, smiling uneasily as my brother spoke our language.

She thanked him in Akkadian, dusting herself off. It took everything I had to *not* try again to smack Massarym, but I knew I would just look spiteful and immature. I couldn't think of anything to say or do, so I said "I'm sorry" in Akkadian.

Massarym glanced from me to Aya. He nodded and grunted as if he understood. The faker.

"Don't worry, Karai," she said. "Your brother tries so hard to make a fool of you. It's not an attractive quality in him. You're considerate and easy to talk to . . . even if you almost smacked me in the nose by accident. Don't let him get under your skin so, Karai."

"Yes, agreed, absolutely," Massarym said. "Heed her word, Brother."

"*Lillu*," I said. *Dunce, dummy.*

"*Lillu*," Aya said, biting back a laugh.

"*Lillu*," Massarym repeated, nodding his head wisely.

Aya and I broke down laughing. Massarym, not knowing what to do, joined in, slapping his knee and guffawing.

The sound of distant thunder rumbled off to the west. I looked over just in time to see one thin line of lightning dart from the sky to the top of the Great Onyx Circle.

Sunday

AYA AND HER family are gone. I'm going to miss her, but I don't have room to think about that now. My faith in my scientific ability is severely shaken.

Our family waved the Akkadians off from the pier, and Aya stood on the deck of the gigantic ship. As they pulled away, the score of oarsmen rowing with all their might, I swear she returned my gaze. I craned my neck as if it would make it easier for her to see me.

When the ship was headed out of the harbor, we climbed into our carriage and rode back to the palace. As we entered the courtyard, a man and woman came into view. They were gesturing wildly, the woman on her knees, the man holding something in his arms. It looked like an enormous bundle of clothes. The courtiers rushed toward them to clear the way, but I bade them stop.

I realized the couple were Lady Karissa and Lord Al'duin. And they were holding a slumped, unconscious Nelik.

As Father, Mother, Massarym, and I leaped out of the carriage and ran to their side, the guards snapped to attention. "Go alert the doctors!" Father commanded. "Run, men!"

As they obeyed, Father hoisted Nelik into his arms and we all followed.

My cousin was a horrible sight to behold. His arms were jerking in spasms, his eyes rolled back into his head, his lips flecked with vomit. With each of Father's steps, Nelik's head bounced awkwardly.

I silently begged him to be all right, for this not to be my fault. Could it have been my blood therapy that caused this? I hadn't experienced any negative symptoms. Neither had Kav'i the vizzeet.[19] No, this had to be something different.

The doctors laid Nelik down on a stretcher. The master doctor, an old man named Kaion, shot terse questions at Nelik's parents. What had he eaten? What had he drunk? Had he ever had an episode like this before?

Lady Karissa was beside herself as she turned from the doctors to Father and Mother. "He—Massarym—he was restored after his fall, was he not? The orb healed him. Please, bring it. Use it on my son or he will die!"

Tears flew nearly horizontally out of her wild eyes.

19 Aside from his usual craziness.

Father held her, almost as much for her sake as for the doctors' safety. "The Loculi are . . . not here," Mother said in a low voice. "It would take hours to fetch them. Will that be enough time?"

As one, the doctors shook their heads no. Lady Karissa let out a long moan and fell to the ground, weeping.

The doctors strapped Nelik's arms to his sides, put a thick piece of cloth in his mouth, and tucked a pillow under his head. As they pulled a leather strap over his forehead, the veins in his neck bulged.

"What are you doing to him?" Lord Al'duin demanded.

"We don't know what caused this seizure. We must keep him from hurting himself." Kaion looked up at us. "All we can do is pray he rides this out."

"Is there no m-medicine?" I asked. "No treatment?"

In answer, Kaion simply shook his head. Mother grabbed my arm and pulled me into a hallway, away from the others. "What did you do?" she hissed, her jaw clenched.

"Mother . . . ?" I said, bewildered.

"Nelik was with you just a few days ago. He was in your lab, and you two were playing scientist. You performed some crazy experiment on him, didn't you?"

"No!" I turned away. "Yes. B-B-But this experiment is safe. I know because I have done it to m-m-myself—"

"Oh, you foolish boy," Mother said. "You are far, far too young to have someone's life on your conscience. A small discovery doesn't mean you have everything figured out. Science is dangerous!"

I glared at her, meeting her fury with my own. "And *your* science, M-M-Mother? Lightning above the Great Onyx Circle? What is that, and why does it occur when the L-Loculi are removed?"

"We are looking into that," she replied.

"Your experiments are making Atlantis itself sick!" I said. "For all I know it's *your* fault this is happening to N-N-Nelik!"

"Karai! Stop!"

Mother's face looked carved from stone. We stood there for a moment, staring into each other's eyes. Then she released her grip on my arm. "Just tell me what happened."

Before I could reply, Father burst through the door, his face bright with relief. "Why did you two disappear like that?"

"Nelik. Is he . . . ?" I asked.

"Alive." Father nodded. "Praise the gods, the fit is over!"

"So quickly!" Mother said, her face flush with relief.

"Kaion was wise to let it run its course," Father said. "It may have been poison from spoiled food. Come. Lady Karissa and Lord Al'duin are asking for you."

As he left, Mother held me back. "This is a stroke of luck, Karai. I have no idea what you're doing in that lab—"

"But Kaion s-s-said—" I protested.

"There was no spoiled food," Mother said. "You will make sure your cousin is cured from whatever this is. And there will be no more experiments, no more crazy theories, no more supervromaskis. Enough is enough."

"What about the g-g-griffin?" I spluttered. "You saw what a great devel . . . development that was—my discovery protecting yours—"

"I thanked you for the griffin, and I meant it," Mother said. "After what we've just seen, let us hope the animal does not get sick and die unexpectedly. Now, let us visit your cousin."

Nelik was curled up on his side, already asleep, breathing normally. His parents were holding each other, his mother quietly sobbing into her husband's chest. Father was sitting by the cot, patting Nelik's shoulder. He didn't notice our arrival, but instead motioned Kaion over.

"L-Look at this," he said, pointing to the back of Nelik's neck.

The doctor parted Nelik's thick dark hair, revealing a strange patch that had turned white.

The bird formation. The Greek lambda.

My hand instinctively reached back to touch the matching shape that had appeared in my own hair.

And that, dear Diary, was when I knew Mother was right.

* * *

Tuesday morning

This morning I rose before the sun.

Sleep was elusive. I dreamed of hundreds of children, lined up at the Parade Grounds, all turned away from me, and on each of their heads was a white Λ. I woke again and again in pools of my own sweat. Mother's voice in my head, scolding me, *This is your mess. Clean it up.*

The courtyard outside is striped with the first rays of the day's sunrise. I want to sneak down and check on Nelik, but I know Mother's probably awake. Her hearing is scarily good and her chambers are on the way to the royal hospital.

Massarym's door just creaked open!

Why is he up so early? Where is he going? Massarym doesn't *ever* get up early.

Footsteps down the hall. He's hurrying. I'll write again this afternoon, I'm going to follow him.

Tuesday, a burrow in the woods around the Great Onyx Circle

DIARY, IS THE world turning upside down?

Seconds ago, a huge crack of thunder exploded in the air directly above my head. A second later it started to rain sheets of water.

I will wait it out here and let you know what has happened.

I saw Massarym heading for the ridge, the Great Onyx Circle. But rather than follow him on my own and risk getting lost, I stopped to retrieve Kav'i. We left the palace perhaps twenty minutes after Massarym. Just as we were in sight of the entrance to the maze, the sky suddenly darkened over the ridge—again, just as it had during the display of Loculi!

What on earth was Massarym doing?

I thought of Mother's words: *The Telion has massive power and comes from the very center of the earth. And we do not understand everything about it. So we must take precautions.*

Precautions. Not exactly Massarym's strength.

The temperature has plummeted, Diary. As I try to keep these pages dry, Kav'i's teeth are chattering with the cold. Unfortunately my cloak is back at the palace. I can't see much from here, but it does seem like this storm has spread. I'm hearing rolls of thunder from the east, above the forest by the Parade Grounds. Bolts of lightning knife through the dark clouds there, lighting up the trees bright as day.

A huge blast of thunder, nearly instantaneous after a blinding flash of lighting. Right above us again. And then—a dark shape in the sky, illuminated by the bolt.

Massarym.

I screamed his name, but there was no way he could

hear me. Maybe if there were a Loculus of Loud Voice he would. With a deep breath I bellowed again, "MAS-SARYM!" What is he doing, toying with the Loculus of Flight during such a storm? This could kill him.

Another huge bolt of lightning, barely missing my brother. Kav'i is screeching, poor thing. Why isn't Massarym coming down? He obviously sees the lightning.

No.

It can't be.

What a fool!

A line of five lightning bolts, quickly in succession like fingers drumming on a table, just followed Massarym through the sky. He dipped and sped away from them, his laugh echoing dully through the thick air.

He is *laughing*.

I am watching him loop through the sky as if baiting the storm. Dear Diary, this is unimaginable! A finger of lightning snakes toward him, curving through the sky, missing him by a finger's breadth. It is as if the lightning is seeking him out. As if the sky itself is sick and must destroy what caused it to happen. As if my crazy twin brother Massarym is an invader to be shot down.

Our island is seizing just like Nelik, every time we remove the Loculi from the Great Onyx Circle.

I cannot stay.

* * *

Later Tuesday

IT WAS STILL pouring rain when Massarym returned to his rooms. I was standing on the balcony we share, watching the downpour. He didn't notice me as he tiptoed in, quietly summoned the maid, and gave her his soaking tunic. "This is our secret, Nilda, right?" he said. "Mother doesn't need to know I was traveling in the rain."

The stout old woman sniffed and marched out of the room. When she was gone, I came in through the open balcony doors.

Massarym gave a visible start when he saw me.

"You were out there? What a storm!" he said, yawning. "The rain woke me up."

"The rain woke you up?" I repeated.

"Yes."

"Just now?"

"That's right." Massarym scratched the back of his neck. "You just spoke twice without s-s-stuttering, brother. What happened?"

"You're scratching your neck, Mass," I said. "You always do that when you're lying."

"And when I have an itch," Massarym said. "Your sleepiness may have eased your tongue, but it has also given you a sour disposition."

As he moved toward his bedchamber, I spoke plainly.

Massarym was right. My words were clear and strong now. "You did it. I saw you flying around, playing with lightning."

Massarym turned, the cocky grin gone from his face. "So what? It's a stormy day, I was having a bit of fun."

"It wasn't a stormy day until you started using the Loculi," I said. "The sun was strong this morning."

"What are you saying, that I caused the storm?" He let out a snort. "And you're a scientist? Storms happen. Weather changes. All that studying has rotted your brain, dear brother. You need to get out more."

He turned again, but I grabbed his arm. "Listen to me, Massarym. The Loculi should never have been constructed. They're disturbing the Telion, throwing the island out of balance."

"So what shall we do, throw them in the ocean?" Massarym retorted.

"I'm not sure," I said. "But we cannot keep removing them."

"Then you will be quite disappointed that I have convinced Mother and Father to have one last display," Massarym replied. "Tomorrow afternoon."

"Another? So soon?" I blurted. "We had two already!"

"There is an unstoppable demand!" Massarym said. "The people ask, so we must comply. As we speak, the heralds are already spreading out into the countryside. This time, we will be using all seven Loculi."

I could not believe this. "We must cancel!" I said.

Massarym wheeled to face me. His eyes blazed. "You have used the Loculi. Did you not feel how it made your blood sing to have that power in your hands? Do you have blood there at all, Karai, or is it just ink and dust?"

And with that, he tore free of my grip, went into his bedchamber, and slammed the door.

Wednesday

THE STORM HAS passed. The sky is an expanse of blue; the plants in the gardens are blooming ecstatically, throwing reds, deep oranges, emerald greens, and silky whites all over the grounds.

The exhibition is scheduled in three hours. I am praying, Diary. Praying that I am wrong. That the weather will stay the same.

That my brother is right and I'm a fool.

I never thought that the possibility of that statement's truth would make me so happy.

Wednesday evening

WHILE IT IS still safe, I must write what I saw today. It may be the last time I can. If this book survives, please, dear reader, wherever—*whenever*—you may be, take heed. Read closely.

This morning, I chose patience over action. I planned only to observe, as any good scientist would. I hoped that my theory about the removal of the Loculi would be proven false. At the exhibition I vowed to dutifully fly here and there using one Loculus. Father would beat a squad of ten elite guards using another. Massarym would disappear and reappear all over the place. And so on and so forth.

That was the plan.

We waited at the Parade Grounds. The stands were thronged with people, easily three times the attendees of the previous exhibition. The smell of roasting meat and candied nuts and figs wafted across the green, manicured field. I noticed, though, that the crowd seemed uneasy. Many faces were solemn or even scowling. I didn't like the air of tension. Glancing at my father, I could see that he felt it, too.

We stood in the very center and waited for the Loculi.

Seven burly soldiers emerged from the tunnel underneath the stands, carrying a litter upon which the Loculi rested, covered in an ornate cloth, stitched with designs that mimicked the filigreed patterns on the orbs themselves. The men set it down on a raised platform, and Mother stepped forward.

In the center of the amphitheater, her voice rang to the back rows.

"People of Atlantis! Within each of you lies something great and mysterious given to you by our cherished Telion, which is known to people all over the world as the Atlantean Force! In front of you now see the concentration of that force, in these seven globes which we, your royal family, will forever use to keep you safe, prosperous, and healthy. Behold!"

The soldiers pulled the cloth off the seven Loculi. They pulsed with a faint light, blue and silver and continually shifting. I looked up at the sky.

Not a cloud in sight.

I thanked the gods, Diary. I was thrilled to have been wrong.

Seeming to sense my unease, Massarym turned and winked at me.

"Today we will show you even more marvels!" Mother continued. "But beyond that: today you, our beloved citizens—without whom there would be no Atlantis, no Telion, and no Loculi—*you* will get a chance to share in our delight!"

A throaty cheer rose from the crowd.

Mother focused her eyes on a withered, elderly woman several rows up, who was sitting with what must have been her family. "Grandmother! Tell me, are you well today?"

A murmur of curiosity rolled through the crowd. The woman knew she was being spoken to, but instead of answering, she merely clung to the young man sitting next to her. I assumed he was her grandson.

"Please, if it's not too painful for her, would you bring her down here?" Mother gestured to our men, who hurried up to the woman's seat. They and her grandson gently helped her down to the field. Her back was painfully bent and she walked with a great deal of difficulty, using an olive-branch cane.

Mother's eyebrows rose as the woman approached. "Oh, dear. I beg your pardon that I called you *grandmother*. Why, I can tell you're not as old as you seem. And so this young man must be . . . your son!"

At first I thought this was idle flattery, but upon closer look I realized she was correct. The woman had the skin, the eyes, the hair of a young mother. She been aged by sickness.

Mother took the sick woman's hand. "You have been very ill for a long time, Mother, and it's not getting better, is it?"

The woman shook her head, tears in her eyes. Mother led her to a stool and bade her sit and be easy. Then she strode to the platform and picked up the pale blue Loculus with the swirling gold patterns on it.

An absolute silence settled over the amphitheater.

Mother held the Loculus in one hand and laid her other hand on the woman's shoulder. Suddenly the woman slumped into the young man's arms. More murmurs from the crowd as the ball began to pulse with a blue glow. After a few moments the woman's eyes fluttered open. She began coughing, then hacked an ugly wad of phlegm onto the grass.

"Now rise before your queen," Mother said.

The woman stopped coughing and took a deep breath. She straightened her back and planted her feet on the ground. Slowly, tentatively, she stood, dropping her cane to the ground.

A gasp rippled through the crowd as she took a few shaky steps—and then a full turn, like a dancer. The expression of shock registered on her face before she threw her arms around her son, both of them openly weeping as the crowd of Atlanteans erupted in wild cheering.

I, too, was swept up in the excitement. I fought back tears. There was no denying that Mother had just used the power of the Loculi to do a great good. Was I mistaken in thinking the things were evil?

Massarym nudged me. "Go grab a girl," he said with a grin. "Take her for a flying lesson."

Before I could respond, he thrust the Loculus of Flight into my hands and pushed me forward, toward Mother. "My queen, you are truly a miracle worker!" he bellowed. "Let us celebrate. My brother—the handsome, dashing, and brilliant Prince Karai—is too shy to speak for himself. Is there a young lady here who would like, for a fleeting moment, to experience the excitement of flying through the air like an eagle—in the arms of Atlantis's most eligible bachelor? I'm not saying you'll be the next princess . . . but who knows?"

Laughter rippled through the crowd as Massarym pointed to a pretty girl, about our age, and beckoned her. Her parents, stunned, made no attempt to stop this.

Taking her hand, Massarym guided her arm around my waist and patted us both on the arm. "Have fun up there," he said.

"I'm so sorry," I said to the poor, confused girl, "but my brother—"

"He's nervous, everyone!" Massarym shouted, turning to the crowd with a smile. He was met with torrents of cheers and encouragement, applause and laughter. And I noticed the young lady was looking at me with disappointment.

He'd outmaneuvered me. I had no choice. "What is your name?" I asked.

"Siasan," she replied.

"I'm Karai," I said.

She laughed. "Of course. We are both being bullied. But I am curious. Can you truly fly?"

I held her around the waist. "Please hold on tight."

As we left the ground, she screamed. A deafening cheer rose from the crowd and quickly fell away as we entered the thin, clear sky.

"Oh!" Siasan exclaimed.

I didn't know if it was an expression of fear or exhilaration, but as I turned I saw a brilliant smile on her face. She was an adventurous one.

I flew back down to the level of the top of the grandstands, where people could see us well, and looped around a few times, carefully holding Siasan with one arm and the Loculus with the other.

"Higher! Please!" Siasan breathed into my ear.

Honestly, Diary, I was having great fun myself. "Ha ha! You see, my blood is *not* made of ink and dust!" I cried out.

"What?" she said.

"Never mind!" I turned and zoomed upward into the cloudless blue sky.

That's when my entire body shook to a distant boom. Out of the corner of my eye, I saw the sky begin to change.

The air itself seemed to be bending, gathering in on itself as if reeled in by a giant invisible hand.

The hairs on the back of my neck stood on end as an impossibly thin, blindingly bright bolt of lighting snaked out of the bruised sky—right toward Siasan and me.

I didn't think. I flipped around and shot westward. Wind whistled past me. My ears popped and rang. Siasan fainted.

And I felt her limp body slide out of the curve of my arm.

Down. Now.

As I began to plummet myself, another boom nearly knocked me loose. I struggled to hold on to the Loculus myself. When I regained purchase, Siasan was far below me, screaming.

Faster!

I dove back toward the earth, but there was no way even the Loculus of Flight would reach her. She was going to die, and all because of me.

But out of the transparent air, a figure appeared below her—Mother! Holding her arms wide, she managed to catch the girl firmly. The impact was jarring but it lasted only an instant before both were gone again from sight.

A moment later they were on the ground, falling ungracefully from each other, but very much alive. My heart beat furiously.

The Loculus of Zap.

If Mother had not thought to use the Loculus of Teleportation—if she had not known how to manipulate it so well—Siasan would be dead. Filled with gratitude and relief, I sped downward and landed moments later.

The spectators were stone silent. Mother glared at me. Then she stood, helping Siasan to her feet. The girl collapsed into Mother's arms, sobbing. Her family surged forward, clambering onto the field, pushing their way past the soldiers. Siasan's eyes rolled back in her head and her body began shaking.

Mother reached for the Loculus of Healing. "Please, everyone, give her some air! She's going to be all right—"

"Siasan!" Her mother grabbed her out of the queen's arms. Mother stepped away, shocked. "Oh, are you offended, Queen Qalani?" the woman snapped. "I don't care who you are! Look what you did to my daughter! Get your awful stones away from her!"

"Some queen! You almost killed that girl!" a voice from the crowd shouted.

"But—but I—" Mother sputtered.

"She *saved* the girl!" Father bellowed.

"The power belongs to the gods, not you!" another voice shouted.

More angry voices began piling up on top of one another until I couldn't make out one jeer from another. I was seized with shock. No one had ever addressed the royal family this way.

Then something hit me on the side of the head. A shoe, thrown from the crowd. A half-eaten skewer of lamb landed at Mother's feet.

Food, shoes, and rotten vegetables began flying through the air toward us.

"PEOPLE! ATLANTEANS!" Father cried out, jumping in front of Mother and batting away a rotten melon. "PLEASE, LISTEN! I COMMAND THAT THERE WILL BE NO MORE GAMES!"

The shouts simmered, but people stopped throwing things. It was Mother the scientist, not Father, who was associated with the Loculi in the people's minds.

"IT IS OUR JOB TO HONOR, DEFEND, AND PROVIDE FOR ALL OF YOU!" he continued, but Mother pulled him away.

"Uhla'ar, what are you saying?" she hissed, her expression neutral to avoid looking emotional in public.

"Qalani, please, hear me, hear your people," Father said softly. "This is wrong. Your achievements in science are immense, but now it's time for you to listen to *me*."

"You?" Mother said calmly. "You who were not born into the royal family, who grew up as one of *them*, until a starry-eyed princess plucked you from obscurity—"

"I earned my station, Qalani!" Father said. "But I am also a brother of the people and they know this. Hear them. Hear their unhappiness."

"They certainly are wondering what we're saying, my dear," Mother said.

"Please, Qalani," Father pressed on, "let's take these Loculi and secure them deep underground, to be used only in times of great—"

A good-sized fish, glistening and still flopping, hit him in the head.

"PLEASE, MY PEOPLE, DO NOT BE ANGRY!" Father announced.

Another fish fell to the ground next to me, bucking and flapping in the grass—still alive. How odd this was. People had brought live fish with them? The creatures had not died from lack of water?

I looked around at the crowd. Their faces were looking upward now. Toward the sky.

They were not throwing fish at all. The fish were falling from above.

Another hit me, then another. I heard a clap of thunder, and the air suddenly became thin and cold. The ground vibrated under my feet, rattling the entire Parade Grounds and the stadium seats.

And then hundreds, thousands of fish were falling from the sky, pouring down like rain.

"Down, Karai, down!" Massarym said. "Someone is bombarding us!"

"Not someone," I murmured.

"Than what?" Massarym shouted. "A griffin with a sick sense of humor?"

"No," I said. "Atlantis."

Our soldiers wrestled us all to the ground, shielding us with their bodies until the grisly storm was over. I could hear panicked screams. People were lamenting the end of the world. But by the time we emerged, the stands were empty of people.

Working together, stepping through the writhing, dying fish, Father and I scooped up the orbs and used the Loculus of Teleportation to return them to the Great Onyx Circle.

Massarym was right. The pain of using this Loculus was nearly unbearable. Groaning as we recovered, we set them into the Heptakiklos.

Immediately afterward, the ground stopped shaking.

We trudged back. At the palace now, the soldiers are still working to remove the fish. Their smell is beginning to permeate every corner. I hope the rain will take care of that, because the skies have opened up even more. I am hearing reports that the rivers and streams have risen dangerously high.

I know that Mother understands the danger of the Loculi now. How could she not? But she will not speak of it. Neither, of course, will Massarym. I dare not speak to Father, or whatever we say will get back to Mother.

I can foresee nothing but tragedy as long as the Loculi exist.

There is only one way out of this, Diary. If it's not already too late.

Tonight I do what must be done.

Years later

MY DIARY! I have found you! I heard murmurings about a book written in a strange tongue that nobody could recognize.

It could have been anything, but I knew.

Somehow I knew.

I have just reread all of what I'd written as a young man. Such naïveté! Such idealism! Well, I admit I am still the same man, albeit older, and I am drawn to continuing what I started.

So, dear Diary, here is what happened. Please be prepared, old friend—for after I tell you I must destroy you, so you do not end up in the wrong hands. You see, nowadays I am living a life untethered to my former self.

The better to track down my brother, Massarym, and what he stole.

Now then. The night of the fish storm, I sneaked through the rain to the Great Onyx Circle and found my way to Mother's beloved Heptakiklos, where the seven deadly Loculi rested.

By now, dear Diary, perhaps you have forgotten the circular ridge, which has since risen up to form the proper volcano known as Mount Onyx. Now the maze through the woods has become a labyrinth through a mountain. But to my story!

I sought my pet vizzeet—what was his name?—Kav'i! Kav'i had vanished from his cage during the chaos of the day. So I was on my own in the maze.

I remember the spring was especially full, glowing with wisps of bluish smoke that seemed to have a luminescence of their own. When I reached the waterfall I stopped to plunge my hands deep, splashing some on my face. It was cold and revitalizing.

Pinpricks of mist dotted my skin as I approached the Heptakiklos.

Eephus—the griffin I had trained painstakingly to protect my mother's invention—was sleeping next to it. He raised his fearsome head, instantly alert as I approached. I spoke gently to him, murmuring reassurance as I moved toward the very objects he was supposed to protect.

Rain pelted me as I stepped closer. The Heptakiklos was dark under the overcast sky, but the Loculi glowed faintly with their own power, and were further lit by the thick streams of blue vapor that issued from cracks all around us.

The Loculi rested in their indentations—but only six glowing spheres. Had the Loculus of Invisibility completely vanished? Before I'd been able to see its flowing energy. The handle of a sword was wedged deep into the middle of the Heptakiklos. I bent down to pick up the invisible orb. My hand touched . . . nothing.

With the Loculus of Invisibility, as you know, one can feel the surface, and then one becomes invisible. But no, Diary—nothing was there!

Behind me the air shifted imperceptibly. In that moment I knew exactly what had happened.

I stood and turned. "M-M-Massarym?"

"A pity, I thought you'd lost that stutter," my brother's voice rang out. "You are terrible at secret plots too, Karai. While you sneaked here, f-f-fumbling and b-b-bumbling your way, I woke Mother and told her of your plans. Do you know what? She didn't want me to throw you and Father in jail for treason against the Crown, where you should be! She argued *for* you, Karai." Massarym laughed bitterly. Two quick footsteps sounded on the stone floor and then I felt my arm being twisted behind my back.

My heart pounded in my chest. I chose not to struggle against him, knowing he was the stronger of us. My thoughts raced. Mother had defended me? I took comfort in that. Perhaps she'd come around.

My shoulder was beginning to throb. "I will go f-freely, Massarym. Let us approach Mother together. Please p-p-put the Loculus back—"

"I'm afraid I can't do that," Massarym said, tightening his grip on my arm. "And I'm afraid a meeting with Mother is not in the plan."

"But—"

"I went looking for you, but you were nowhere on the continent," Massarym said. "Clever, eh? You think you're the smart one, brother, because you love books, because you used magic and wizardry to teach yourself Akkadian, but *you're not.*"

Sharp pain stabbed through my shoulder.

"My brother, the power is changing you," I said, "but you must come to your senses. This is not a question of who is smarter—"

Massarym's hand shoved me down to one knee. "I heard you and Father, acting like holy men, pretending you *know anything* about Mother's invention. You think the Loculi are responsible for the weather, for the flying fish? Well, you may be right, you may be wrong, but think, Karai. You're a scientist. What does a scientist do but refine and change? The Loculi are a *work in progress.* And you cannot stop progress!"

"What does Mother say now, Massarym?" I pleaded. "Have you spoken to her after what happened this afternoon?"

"I have told her you want to destroy the Loculi," Massarym plowed on. "She said this was an act of treason. And she asked me to come after you."

"Mother would not have said that!" I shouted, struggling to free myself. "Traitors to Atlantis are killed. She knows I just want to protect us all!"

"What is the matter, sad that you won't be king?" Massarym said. "You expected to lead a nation after such a traitorous plan?"

He was a madman. The Loculi had changed him. In my panic I was seeing things with extreme clarity.

Massarym hadn't spoken to Mother at all. Of course. She wouldn't have sent him alone to get me. If she had really wanted to stop me, she would have come herself.

Nobody knew we were here. Which was terrifying.

I jumped into action, kicking at the mass behind me, guessing where Massarym's legs were. I heard a thump and a cry and my arm was free! I swung my arms wildly at the patch of air that was my brother, connecting again and again. Then my hand hit something hard, and Massarym popped into view. I heard the soft thud of the Loculus landing invisibly on the floor. I saw the slight, slick furrow in the mud as it rolled away.

"Ah well, at least my hands are free," Massarym said with a grin as he lunged at me.

He was far stronger, Diary. As he grabbed me, I twisted in his grip, trying to knee him or butt him with my head.

My fists pummeled the air helplessly as he squeezed my arms to my side. He shoved me backward to the wall of the cave, when my foot hit something, something round—the invisible Loculus! I stumbled over it and lost my balance. As my brother and I fell to the ground, my head hit stone, and everything went black.

I don't remember how much time went by before I came to, with a throbbing pain in my head. It felt like the earth was moving beneath me.

I blinked my eyes and realized the earth *was* moving beneath me.

Nevertheless I struggled to my feet and swung my arms around, trying to find Massarym, trying to continue the fight that was unfortunately long over. "Show yourself and fight me, you coward!" I screamed.

Then I saw the Heptakiklos. It was completely empty.

All seven Loculi gone.

"Massarym?"

My heart rose to my mouth. I scanned the area helplessly. I don't know how long I was out, but it was still dark and still raining. As I tried to think what to do, a violent tremor shook the earth and I fell to my knees.

Eephus the griffin trumpeted in panic. He shifted his weight from side to side, extending and folding his gigantic wings. His eyes rolled back in his head like a panicked horse. That Massarym managed to evade the beast somehow did not surprise me.

A massive creaking noise echoed above me, and I looked up to see a gigantic rock tip slowly from the top of the great ridge, which seemed at least ten feet higher than it had been moments ago.

"Eephus!" I cried out. The creature looked up and tried to fly away, but the rock rolled down the ridge and pinned his right wing to the floor.

He screeched in pain, flapping his opposite wing and scrabbling against the boulder with his talons. I ran to him, looking into his huge eyes, which were wide with terror. I spoke soothing words, trying to calm him. I reached a hand out to the wounded wing, and with a cry he lashed out with his beak, slicing into my arm. As I leaped away, the beast snapped at me, straining against the boulder.

The next rock that fell was in flames, and it landed in a patch of scrub that was dry enough to catch fire.

The ground shook again. The ridge lurched upward like a growing creature. A crack appeared in the ground, opening into a black chasm. I had to leave the area or I knew I would die.

I wanted to save the griffin. I racked my brain about ways to dislodge it and drag it away.

Don't be foolish. Save yourself, or you'll both die.

"I have to go, Eephus," I said. "I'm sorry."

As I ran for a little-used tunnel, I heard a shriek and

looked over my shoulder. Eephus had ripped his wing out from under the massive boulder. He was following me, dragging the injured wing at his side. There was nothing but fury in his eyes.

No time to think. I sped away, bleeding, hearing Eephus's screams behind me. I nearly fell into a hidden hole. A spring-loaded arrow missed my head by inches. Where had that come from?

I ignored the maze that had been cut through the forest. My ankles were lashed with thorns as I ran blindly toward the opposite side of the ridge. Toward home.

As I emerged into the flat lands, I tripped on a root and fell.

With a snort, Eephus emerged from the forest behind me. He was not alone.

My jaw dropped open. Trees were tilting left and right, crashing down hard on the soaked soil. From their midst came a creature like nothing I'd seen before. It seemed to be gaining mass from the soil, the roots and trunks and leaves themselves—a face, mouth, a ring of eyes that billowed and bulged into an amorphous mass of glowing green. It groaned as it grew, casting its cold, hungry eyes in all directions.

What on earth was this thing of horror? What had we unleashed in our foolish quest for power? I did not want to know.

Eephus screeched, half running on its spindly legs, half

flying. I ran away, toward the safety of the kingdom. Above me I saw a great swooping bird.

No. It was no griffin but Massarym, heading downward for me.

I felt him grab my shoulder and I was lifted upward. In the dim moonlight I saw a sack around his shoulders. "Th-thank you!" I shouted.

He did not reply. Instead he carried me up . . . up . . . until the tops of the trees were far beneath us. Now safely in the distance, I could see the green mountain creature making a swath of destruction through the jungle. Fireballs fell from the sky as if thrown by the gods themselves. As we swung over the harbor I could see the ships rocking placidly in their moorings.

"I—I'm sorry," Massarym said, and before I could ask him to explain, he let me go.

I remember falling. I remember thinking I was going to die. I know I woke up floating in the sea and commandeering a ship with the first wave of Atlanteans who fled the destruction. And I remember seeing the fireball that fell like a planet, consuming Atlantis in flames before my eyes.

I've been told ours was the only surviving ship, but I hope this is not true.

Please forgive me, Diary, for not being able to write more. It is a vision quite too painful to remember.

I still do not know how you ended up here, Diary, in

the land of the Phoenicians, where I have taken refuge. Is it possible my mother or father survived with a few choice mementos? Will I find them? I wish you could tell me!

Well.

~~There is a knock at the door. I hear my name being~~ called. Maybe this . . .

By the gods, Diary, I know this voice.

Could it be?

Or is my brother just heavy on my mind now?

Let me check. I will return in—

[Editor's note: This is where the text ends. A search is ongoing for any other remnants of the writing of Karai of Atlantis.]

READ A SNEAK PEEK OF BOOK FIVE

the LEGEND of the RIFT

CHAPTER ONE

FIRST DAY OF THE END OF THE WORLD

YOU KNOW YOU'VE reached rock bottom when you're standing on a beach, looking to the horizon, and you don't notice you're ankle-deep in dead fish.

If I'd been there ten minutes earlier, the water would be up to my shoulders. Now I was at the top of a wet, sloping plain. It was littered with rocks, ropes, bottles, crabs, fish, a massive but motionless shark, and the rotted hull of an old shipwreck.

Our tropical island had shot upward like an express elevator. Ten minutes ago, King Uhla'ar of Atlantis had opened a rift in time, which according to legend would make the great continent rise again. But I wasn't really thinking about legends right then. Because when he jumped into that

1

rift, he took Aly Black with him. One minute there, the next minute *boom*! Down and gone. Back into time. Back to Atlantis.

Losing Aly was like losing a part of myself.

So on the first day of the end of the world, I, Jack McKinley, felt like someone had reached down my throat and torn out my heart.

"Jack! Marco! Cass! Eloise!"

Mom.

I spun around at her voice. She was back on the sandy part of the beach, glancing over her shoulder. Behind us, a group of frightened Massa soldiers streamed out of the jungle. Marco Ramsay, Cass Williams, and his sister, Eloise, were standing at either side of me. And that was when I began to notice the fish. Because a really ugly one whipped my left ankle with its fin.

"They look nasty," Eloise said.

"They speak highly of you," Cass replied.

Eloise looked at him, completely baffled. "Who, the Massa?"

"No, the fish," Cass said. "Aren't you talking about the—"

"I'm talking about *those* guys!" Eloise said, pointing to the frantic soldiers. "Do you hear Sister Nancy—I mean, Jack's mom? She's warning us to stay out of their way."

From deep in the trees, I could hear the shrill screech

of a poison-spitting vizzeet—followed by the guttural cry of a soldier in great pain. The Massa headquarters was on the other side of the jungle, and their soldiers and scientists were running here to see what had happened.

They'd felt the rumble, but they had no idea about the rift. And about the monsters who had escaped.

"Aw, man, what a trap," said Marco. "Those critters? They're like, woo-hoo, Greek dinner, free delivery!"

Some of the Massa were laying their bloodied pals on the sand. Others were running in confusion and panic down the muddy, fish-strewn beach toward us. Some were barfing in the reeds, nauseated by the violent motion of the earth. Mom was trying to calm them all down, tell them what had happened in the caldera. She wore a Massa-brown robelike uniform like something from a fashion catalog in 1643. The soldiers respected her, but they didn't know she was (a) my mom and (b) a rebel spy. And Torquin, our beloved seven-foot bodyguard, was directly behind us, picking his nose, which he did when he was nervous.

"We watched Aly go, Jack," Cass said. "What are we going to do?"

It was hard to think. There was another huge problem none of us wanted to talk about—Uhla'ar had taken the Loculus of Strength with him. If we didn't find all seven of the magic Atlantean Loculi, our G7W gene would kill us on schedule by our fourteenth birthdays. So if even one

3

Loculus was missing, we were toast.

The fish were distracting me now, and I pulled us all back onto more solid ground. As we did, the Massa bellowed to each other, mostly in Greek. They were pushing and jostling, positioning themselves to ogle the shipwreck. Fifty or so yards down the muddy slope the ship's remains rose out of the muck like a dinosaur skeleton. It canted to one side, its mast tilted and cracked. Seaweed hung from its crossbeams like long-forgotten laundry, and the wooden hull was lumped with barnacles. Weirdly, after more than a century underwater, the ship's name was still visible on the hull.

The *Enigma*.

"Dudes, call me crazy," Marco said, pushing a couple of the soldiers out of our way, "but you think the answer might be out there, in the ship?"

"You're crazy," Cass said.

Marco's size thirteen feet made slurping sounds in the mud as he stepped toward the ship. "Okay, stay with me now . . . That ship belonged to what's his face, right? The guy who discovered the island in the eighteen hundreds. Marvin or Berman."

"Herman Wenders," Cass said.

"Right," Marco said. "So I'm thinking, we go out there and explore the ruins. Wenders was supposed to be a genius, right? What if he left behind important stuff—you know,

4

maps, notebooks, secrets? I mean, this is the guy that discovered the rift, right? Maybe he knows how to get in and out of it without all the bad consequences."

"We'll be like pirates." Eloise began striding toward the ship with an exaggerated limp. *"Argggh!* Yo-ho-ho, avast and ahoy! Batten the britches! Poop the decks!"

From the look on Cass's face, he wished his long-lost sister were still lost.

Torquin's gloomy expression melted, and he snorted bubbles through his freshly picked bulbous nose. That would be a disturbing sight under normal conditions, but it was worse now. These days he looked like the Hulk dipped into an acid bath. His face was still black with burn marks from a car explosion in Greece, and his once-red hair was just a few blackened clumps. "Ha. She said poop. Funny girl."

"I say we go back to the rift and offer the king a trade," Cass murmured. "We take Aly, he takes Eloise."

Hearing that, Eloise picked up a dead eel and threw it at him. He giggled and ducked. Like typical sibs who'd been fighting all their lives. Which was strange because until recently Cass didn't even know he had a sister. With their parents in jail and their lives scattered among foster families, it was like they needed to make up for lost time.

"So I try to be serious," Marco said with exasperation, "and this is what I get."

"They're blowing off steam," I said. "Trying to be normal."

5

I couldn't blame them. If old Herman Wenders hadn't come to this godforsaken island in the first place, maybe the Karai followers would never have organized the institute. And then no one would have discovered the Atlantean G7W gene that made a superpower out of your biggest talent, but killed you at fourteen. And I would be a normal thirteen-year-old kid in Indiana, worrying about math and sometimes being whomped by Barry Reese. True, I'd be about to drop dead, but at least I'd be blissfully ignorant about that. And I wouldn't have wasted all these past weeks looking for seven Loculi to cure us—which we now knew we would never find. And Aly would still be here.

But he had, and they did, and it was, and I'm not, and we did, and she isn't. So in four months I would be an ex-Jack, the G7W Kid with No Talent.

I wondered if I'd have a chance to say good-bye to my dad. Was he still in the airport in Greece, where we'd left him? Would I ever be able to contact him?

"Earth to Jack?" Cass said.

I looked around into the mass of confusion. "Okay, if we do nothing, we're dead," I said. "The Massa are up in a twist about the earthquake and the ship. That won't last forever. They're going to turn on us. Marco, visiting the ship is a cool idea. But I say we try to get Aly now."

"Us and what army?" Cass said, looking back toward the jungle.

6

Marco puffed out his chest. "Who needs an army when you have Marco the Magnificent?"

"Did you see that . . . *thing* that was stuck in the rift?" Cass said. "It was huge. And . . . and . . . green. And magnificenter than you!"

"You mean the thing that I stabbed, thank you very much?" Marco said.

"Yeah, but what about all those disgusting creatures who escaped? Listen. Just listen!" Cass turned toward the jungle, which echoed with the hooting and cackling of panicked animals. "You see what's been happening to the Massa. There are vizzeets and griffins and vromaskis in there—hundreds of them!"

Marco nodded thoughtfully. "Well, yeah, even human physical perfection has its limits."

"That's the most modest thing I've ever heard you say," Cass said.

"So we'll use the Loculus of Invisibility and the Loculus of Flight. Just pass 'em by. They won't even know we're—" Marco cut himself off in midsentence. "Uh, one of you guys did take the backpack, didn't you?"

Cass shook his head. I shook my head. My heart was dropping like a freight elevator.

"Nope," Torquin added.

"And the shards of the Loculus of Healing?" Marco continued.

"Everything happened so fast—" I said.

Marco put his palm over his face. "Man. I thought I was supposed to be the dumb one! Guess I'll dust off three seats in the doofus corner."

"Five," Torquin said, counting on his sausage-sized fingers. "I mean, four."

A deep rumbling noise cut the conversation short. For a moment I saw two Casses. The ground shook, as if a silent subway train were passing underneath. I bent my knees instinctively. I could hear a distant *crawwwwwk*—the *Enigma* creaking as it shifted with the earth's movement.

Cass held on to Marco. I held on to Torquin. My body lurched left, right, up, down, as if the world itself had slipped on its axis. Every other noise—seagulls, the distant crashing of the surf—stopped.

Then, as quickly as the movement began, it ended.

In the silence, I could hear Brother Dimitrios's voice cry, *"Earthquake!"*

"Duh," Torquin said.

Cass groaned. "Ohhhh, I feel motion sick. The world is about to end and I am going to die in a pile of my own puke."

"Swallow three raw eggs," Torquin said. "Very good for nausea."

"This is just the beginning," Cass moaned. "It's like Aly said. If the rift opened, Atlantis would rise, and the continental plates would shift. Then, *wham*. Tidal waves, earthquakes. New York and LA go underwater. Massive fires sweep the land . . . dust clouds block the sun."

"Cass, we can't panic," I said.

"Don't be a denier, Jack!" Cass said. "This is *exactly* what happened in the time of the dinosaurs—and you know what became of them."

Marco wiped sweat from his brow. "I don't think we have a choice. Jack's right. Face down those critters! *Into the rift*!"

Whenever Marco moved, he moved fast. In a microsecond he was dragging a protesting Cass back up the beach toward the jungle. I followed behind.

A scream greeted us as we got to the tree line. It was loud and human, maybe twenty yards deep into the jungle. It rose to a horrific, pained bellow, then stopped abruptly. I squinted into the trees, dreading what I might see. But even in the brightness of the afternoon sun, the thick treetops cast shadows, making the jungle nearly pitch-dark.

"Wh-wh-who do you think that is?" Cass asked.

"*Was*, from the sound of it," Marco said.

"S-see what I mean?" Cass said, backing away. "Someone just died in there. We could be next. I am staying out here in the light. I'll take goons in robes over human-eating beasts any day."

An acrid stench of rotten flesh wafted out of the jungle, and Cass gagged.

"Whoa. Beans for lunch, Torquin?" Marco said, waving his arms.

"No. A Twinkie," Torquin replied.

I was focusing on a dark shadow in the jungle behind Cass. "Guys . . ." I squeaked. "Look."

Marco's eyes fixed on the black shape. His body tensed. "Cass," he said softly. "Do. Not. Move."

Cass spun around. With a sound that was halfway between an animal roar and the grinding of metal, a hose-beaked vromaski emerged from the jungle shadows. It launched its boar-like body toward Cass. It flexed its claws and its nose tube folded backward, revealing three sets of razor teeth.